SUSANNA
MALCOLM

AN
INCONVENIENT
MATCH

This is a work of fiction. Similarities to real people, places or events, as they occurred or are imagined to have occurred, are entirely coincidental.

AN INCONVENIENT MATCH

First Edition. February, 2019

Copyright © 2019 Susanna Malcolm

For G.,
because every time
I wonder "Should I...",
you say yes.

CHAPTER ONE
&.&

London
1860

Honora Albina Botham solemnly stood at the altar of her wedding ceremony in a costly new blue gown of impeccable, understated elegance. Her bridegroom, Jasper Edward Martin Thorpe, the Earl of Ashland, was contrarily clad in a rumpled, stained garment one could only assume was last night's suit. He reeked of alcohol and tobacco, as well as some god-awful perfume that was likely common to the cheapest of whores. He tottered on his feet and were it not for the censorious stare of the bishop before them, would undoubtedly have collapsed where he stood.

His bloodshot eyes made every effort to focus on the proceedings. This Honora knew because of the incessant way in which he kept squinting and then opening his eyes, and then, as would a disgruntled toddler, rubbing them with a balled fist. Topping one dark eyebrow was a fresh cut, whose healing was made impossible by the aforementioned eye-rubbing. A smear of blood marked his forehead. Honora took a quiet, steadying breath.

There were six people seated in the pews behind her, two of whom were attorneys. The remainder were servants of long-standing Botham family employ.

Among the handful of Ashland's witnesses were three like-clad individuals who seemed to find the proceedings the highest sort of entertainment. They chatted and snickered, and mumbled disjointed responses to the bishop's intonations. Occasionally a cloud of alcohol wafted over from their direction.

The bishop, sensing the way of things, hurried the service along with as much seemly haste as he could muster. It ended rather abruptly, on the bishop's note of open relief as he informed the groom he was free to kiss his bride.

Honora obediently turned to the man who was now her husband and waited. She carried a little nosegay which seemed beside the point, its cheery flowers better suited for more jovial nuptials. Nevertheless, it occupied her uncharacteristically damp hands and she clutched it tightly before her. She looked up at Ashland. He swayed a bit on his feet and then, evidently sensing a lull in the proceedings, looked hastily around. His eyes swept past his bride and landed upon his fellows, who were now laughing with shrill enthusiasm.

"That's done," he said, and without a backward glance left his place at the altar to join them.

* * *

"Well, it's done," her attorney, Mr. Whitmarsh, echoed as he shook her hand. His partner, Mr. Hamersley, nodded in agreement and made a show of not turning around to stare at Ashland and his loutish friends, whose volume had reached a level difficult to ignore.

"Now see here!" the bishop snapped, muting but not suppressing the rowdy conversation.

"...leg-shackled now, old man!" Ashland's friends burst into laughter, a barking sound that echoed coldly off the church walls and put Honora's teeth on edge.

"The earl would seem to be a trifle disguised," Mr. Hamersley commented with an awkward attempt at a smile, earning a snort from his partner. Honora concentrated on smoothing her skirt, a polite motion to cover the fact that she was wiping her palm on her dress. She transferred the nosegay and did the same with her other damp hand. She did not like damp hands nor the attendant implication that they were caused by nerves.

"He's ape-drunk," Mr. Whitmarsh observed, displaying none of his partner's reticence. "Not a sixpence to scratch with and now hanging on your sleeve. Begging your pardon, Honora. Or Lady Ashland, I suppose."

Honora nodded, unfazed by Whitmarsh's candor. He had been her grandmother's attorney, and was used to plain speaking, and it wasn't as if she could disagree with the accuracy of his observation: The earl *was* intoxicated and he *was* insolvent. It was the truth.

The remainder of her guests approached to offer their congratulations. Honora thanked them warmly, happy for the distraction of their familiar faces, most of which had also known her grandmother. As they departed, she glanced over at her new husband and his friends, illuminated in red and gold by a shaft of sunlight coming through the stained-glass behind them, as though they weren't making enough of a spectacle and needed more attention drawn their way. Whitmarsh and Hammersley followed her gaze. "...tenant for life," one of the intoxicated men said with a side-long glance in her direction. "By no less than a bishop! To make sure it sticks!" More guffaws.

Honora watched them for another moment and turned away, wearied by the juvenile display.

"Your grandmother would certainly be pleased to see the matter done," Mr. Hamersley, ever the optimist, interjected.

"Yes, yes," Whitmarsh concurred. "You married and a countess in the bargain. Not even Harriet would have hoped so high."

Honora raised a brow, indicating her doubt. No hope had been too high for her wily grandmother. "You know, Mr. Whitmarsh, that a title was Granny's utmost aspiration for me. I'm certain her greatest regret is not having lived to see it for herself. Though it is a less than...solemn occasion."

Whitmarsh inclined his head, acknowledging her point.

"There will be some paperwork, of course, for you and his lordship to sign. At your leisure, since you will be, er, honeymooning," Mr. Hamersley said with a look of kindly sympathy.

There was a moment's pause during which Honora avoided their eyes, pretending an intense interest in the nosegay. Really, so much kindness on her wedding day for all the wrong reasons could turn a bride glum if she didn't guard against it.

"That should settle it, then," Mr. Whitmarsh said with a glance to the door. "At your leisure, as Hamersley said, m'dear. We will take care of matters as agreed. Shall we see you to the carriage?"

Honora gladly accepted his offer and left the church without a backward glance at Ashland or his friends, their tittering trailing her out the door into the sunshine. She thanked the attorneys again for their presence and their advice, and sank gratefully into the empty carriage, expelling a sigh of relief as the silence settled around her. She leaned her head back against the soft velvet cushion and allowed herself a moment to close her eyes on what had already been a very eventful day.

All things considered, the ceremony had passed as well as one might have hoped. She'd had no illusions, no particular hopes or expectations that would have been dashed by the awkward display inside the church, thus she suffered no disenchantment now. Yet no bride, however levelheaded, could rejoice in a groom so openly reluctant to marry her. And while she did not particularly care what his cronies thought or said of her, the atmosphere inside had been awfully uncomfortable, and she was glad of a moment's solitude before continuing on to the next stage of their journey.

She thought of her grandmother, touching the pendant at her neck. She rubbed the smooth metal of Granny's oldest piece of jewelry, thinking that Granny would have positively exulted if she'd been here to witness the wedding, and she would undoubtedly not have taken the groom's humiliating antics lightly. She'd a way of voicing her opinions, and Honora smiled as she imagined the scathing dressing-down Granny would have delivered to Ashland and his friends.

It was better, perhaps, that Granny weren't here; she never would tolerate disrespect directed at Honora.

Honora's smile faded and she looked down at the pretty little nosegay still clutched in her hands. She lifted it to her nose, and breathed in the sweet floral scent, knowing that the smell of these flowers would always remind her of her wedding day. She leaned over and opened the opposite carriage door, and tossed the silly bouquet swiftly into the street. There was nothing flowers could do for her now. She must remember who she was, and what she had achieved, and proceed accordingly.

It took Ashland another twenty minutes to teeter into the carriage, entering amid a chorus of guffaws and lewd suggestions from his friends, who mercifully chose not to show their faces to Honora. He did not so much as glance at his bride, but kept his eye trained out the window until the carriage rolled away. With a flip he let the curtain down and sprawled back against the cushion across from her, rubbing a hand roughly over his face and hair, making himself even more disheveled than Honora would have thought possible.

Suddenly, his red-rimmed gaze fixed on her, in what was the first time he'd looked directly at her all day. Honora met his look coolly, even something decidedly warm unfurled within her chest and spooled along her spine. She personally felt that his dark-lashed eyes, a mercurial blue-green, were his best feature, and even bleary as he was, his stare succeeded at stirring something within her. His wonderful eyes, alas, were at the moment watching her with no particular tenderness, merely observing her with a shadow of puzzled enquiry. His dark brows drew into a frown and Honora lifted her chin, a habit of old at any hint of scrutiny.

"It will be a cold night tonight, methinks," he sighed, shaking his head. He looked away, as though the idea of it were too much for him. Then, folding his arms across his chest, he closed his eyes, and within minutes his head was lolling to one side, a soft snore issuing from his open mouth.

If anything, it was too warm in the carriage and the weather outside was particularly fine; they would not even need a fire once they reached the inn. Honora shrugged off his comments as a result of intoxication and passed the rest of the journey silently staring out the window, resolutely not being disappointed in their first conversation as man and wife.

CHAPTER TWO

The inn where the newly-wedded couple stopped for the evening was a mediocre place, aged without being charming, and not very tidy, but it was the only inn on the road for miles, and night was quickly falling. They would not make Ashland Park until the following morning.

Honora peered out of the carriage window and disembarked with a mixture of reluctance and eagerness, looking about the place with little curiosity. It had thus far been a long journey, the entirety of which she had spent watching her new bridegroom sleep, his head lolling in time to the swaying of the carriage, one or two of the more jarring bumps along the way eliciting a startled snort.

He sprang out of the carriage behind her, rumpled and red-eyed, and followed her into the public room. There they were met by a distressed innkeeper, who regretted that the best room had already been let to a gentleman from Bath and there was naught he could offer them but a common chamber of humble proportions. Ashland acquiesced with a disinterested nod and requested a private dining room. Honora watched in silent astonishment as he turned without a glance and followed the innkeeper out. What choice did she have but to follow the innkeeper's apologetic wife to the little garret under the eaves, the door of which was so low that she was forced to duck her head to avoid braining herself?

The room was miniscule, hardly big enough to turn around in. The majority of space was taken up by a rickety looking bed, which may or may not have been able to hold more than one occupant. Honora instructed her own maid to unpack only the nightly essentials and store her trunk downstairs.

It was a solitary meal for her, as the arrival of a tray of food indicated that she was not expected, or likely wanted, to join her husband for a meal downstairs.

She ate hurriedly, knowing she must change from her wedding dress to nightgown before Ashland should arrive. A good thing all in all, as the cuisine did not bear savoring, and she was only too happy to send the tray away and let her maid Poppy help her undress.

"That will do, Poppy. You may get yourself to bed, we have another day of travel before us."

Poppy curtsied and smiled with exceptional warmth, her cheeks rosier than usual. She was a happy girl, and thoroughly pleased for what she understood to be her mistress's great day. "Goodnight, miss—my lady! Oh, I will try harder to remember, but I have known you these four years as Miss Honora. It will take some practice."

"Of course it will." Honora smiled. "Do not fret over it. I will dress myself. Have a good night."

"And you, my lady," Poppy said with a parting glance at the bed, leaving with a sigh, though Honora thought it was hardly a bed or room to sigh over.

Honora gazed down at the ivory colored nightdress Poppy had so carefully spread on the bed. It was not overly provocative—a plunging neckline would hardly suit her diminutive chest— but it was the best Italian silk, the fabric so fine and supple that it fell across the body like water, leaving little to the imagination. This she knew, having, in a fit of audacity, tried the thing on when it had been delivered.

How could she wear such a thing before a stranger? In a flash of uncertainty she changed her mind, and decided to settle on a plain linen nightgown, before remembering that Poppy had removed the trunk with all of her belongings. There was nothing for it, but to carry on as planned.

She felt better after putting it on, sensual and flushed. Pretty. She ran her hands down the front of her body. The silk was miraculous, and she made a mental note to order more nightgowns in the same fabric. Full of anticipation, she turned and paced the tiny room, trying to decide how best to present herself to her new husband. Bashfulness made her decide on the bed, which seemed all too obvious but at least offered the benefit of cover-up.

She sat propped against the pillows, blankets at her waist, and awaited the Earl of Ashland to claim his husbandly rights.

The Countess of Ashland. It was certainly one of the most reputable titles in the realm, and Honora had not by any means been the only one pursuing Ashland. But she had been the only one to win him. She smiled at the thought, and the accompanying sense of satisfaction. She was a woman whose grandmother had been born into poverty, but whose son would one day sit in the House of Lords. Still, success had never been certain until they'd met at the altar today; or, more correctly, would not be absolutely certain for a matter of hours, until the thing was consummated.

Honora pressed her palms to her face, astounded at absolutely all of it.

Two hours later, she was fidgety with boredom. And cross. A foolish desire to protect the girl's romantic notions kept her from ringing for Poppy and sending her to enquire after his lordship's whereabouts. Let someone, at least, enjoy the fantasy that this union had anything to do with romance. Honora knew her husband did not love her. In fact, he probably did not even like her. And he undoubtedly had not wanted to marry her.

She wanted it done. Irrevocable. Wedded and bedded, as the old saying went. And if she were honest with herself, as she always tried to be, she yearned to have it done in a very fleshly way that had nothing to do with legalities. In addition to possessing the requisite title—an earldom, no less— she was fortunate in her bridegroom's appearance. It would be fair to say that he was handsome. But to be utterly truthful, it would need to be said that he was young, virile and boldly attractive. Even bedraggled and discourteous as he'd been at the church, she'd felt a spark of attraction for him. She wondered if there were something wrong with her to think so.

Ashland was tall, blue-eyed, dark haired. She knew from the earlier investigation that he enjoyed riding and fencing. He certainly bore the resulting physique, a fit, muscular, manly form that showed no evidence of paunch or physical dissipation. He appeared as well-built as some of the captivating statues she'd seen in Italy.

Under the covers she rubbed her legs together, enjoying the sensation of silk against her sensitive skin. Honora had waited a long time for this night. Sexual congress as an unmarried woman had never been worth the risks: pregnancy, disease, manipulation. No, she had waited. She had waited a good long time.

Yet she wasn't completely ignorant. Honora had, in her practical and purposeful way, discovered a great deal regarding the act of physical love. Owing to the limited discretion of a married friend, as well as several very useful scientific texts, she was aware of the logistics of human joining, how a man came into a woman, what it took for him to reach completion. The real information, however, had come from a very friendly evening spent in the company of one Sylvie Bellerose, an actual courtesan.

Shocking, really, that Honora would stoop to that. Even Granny, so fond of repeating *"Forewarned is forearmed,"* could not approve. But really, Miss Bellerose had been kinder than many so-called respectable *ton* matrons, and her information had been invaluable. Honora could hardly imagine going into a situation such as one's wedding night without being amply informed. It seemed foolish in the extreme to enter such a state of affairs in ignorance. And oh, the information... To this day Honora could hardly credit some of what Miss Bellerose had told her.

She could only hope the things were true. Virtue was not without its toll.

Sometime later, long after most of the candles had burned out, she was awakened by the sound of the door and a heavy step. She sat up, wincing at the ache in her neck that came from sleeping askew, to see Ashland entering the room, drunk, judging by the smell that accompanied him.

He did not appear to notice her. Without speaking he removed his coat, tossing it onto the floor and pulling his shirt out of the waistband. Then he sat and tugged off his boots, letting them fall with a thump. He unbuttoned his shirt and stood and stretched, naked torso glinting in the sputtering candlelight. Honora caught her breath.

He really was most incredibly beautiful. Broad-shouldered, long-limbed and lean, no sign of the stoutness so indicative of the indolent lifestyle of men in his circumstance. Athleticism, energy and youth showed in every sinew and muscle.

An involuntary noise escaped her at the moment when he actually pushed down his trousers. The sound finally succeeded in drawing his attention to her.

Honora could only stare back at him as he looked at her, fighting the urge to bring the blankets to her chin and cover herself. After a long minute he approached the bed, wobbling on unsteady legs. At the jerk of his chin, Honora obligingly moved over.

The bed was so small that he was instantly flush against her, torso to torso, his long legs rubbing against hers. The thin layer of silk whispered between their skin, and Honora closed her eyes at the sensation. Now he would remove the gown, according to Sylvie, and hold her naked form against him. Sylvie had also explained the importance of the initial stages of lovemaking, going into explicit detail regarding touching and kissing. Honora could not help rubbing her legs together in anticipation, for Ashland was so very appealing and must definitely have some expertise in the matter.

She opened her eyes in startled confusion when she felt a damp kiss on her shoulder. He mumbled something, possibly her name, and kissed her wetly on the mouth. He tasted of wine and...cheese? His hand moved to her breast, grasping and caressing her breast through the silky gown. It sent a bolt of heat through her. Honora gasped.

His breath was warm against her neck, an equally incredible sensation. His entire body next to hers was thrilling, all unexplored masculinity, hard angles and rough contours, the hair of his chest unexpectedly grazing her arm. She put her hands upon his shoulders, his skin soft, his muscles firm.

His hand moved downward, over the silky territory of her belly and down toward her hip, where he paused in a wavering caress. Honora's breath caught in her throat, her eyes instinctively following the path of his touch. Her heartbeat tripled. There was a strange coiling in her lower belly at the sight of his dark, thoroughly male hand atop her silk-clad flesh, at the thrill of this intimate contact. She had an urge to push herself against him, to feel everything with an even greater intensity.

But then he moved atop her, tugging the nightgown up about her waist and settling himself between her legs. He reached down, his eyes clenching shut in concentration as he moved against her slowly. She felt movement and a touch between her legs, the back of his hand, or...

"Oh!" She gasped at a sudden sharp stinging pain, and he paused. There was an uncomfortable fullness inside her and after a moment he moved again. The pain was less but still burned considerably. He slid against her and back, every movement producing an odd sensation between her legs, like a pinching inside her. He was heavy atop her, his wine-soaked breath flooding her senses, and she wished he would go back to touching her breast.

Before Honora could even decide where to placed her hands or comprehend the full consequence of his actions, he arched backward and jerked twice against her with a low guttural moan. His head fell against hers, the skin of his forehead warm and damp. He gasped and exhaled, and then pulled off her and slumped back onto the bed. He muttered something, which may have been 'Goodnight' or 'Turn out the light,' shifted once, and was immediately snoring.

Honora, befuddled, stared up at the dim ceiling, her heart thudding madly, foolishly as she tried to catch her breath. Listening to the uninterrupted timbre of her new bedmate, she thought in frustrated bewilderment that Sylvie had been wrong about it all. It hadn't been delightful or pleasant or any of the other things she'd said.

Why, it had been perfectly, disappointingly awful.

CHAPTER THREE

In front of this house, Ash was but a speck. It rose high into the air above him, and likely tunneled into the earth far beneath him. He stood on the top step, tipping his head back as far as he could. *Yes*, he wanted to say, *my insignificance is abundantly clear*. The old stone went up, up, past the point where he could see.

He lowered his head to what he could see, though it wasn't something he particularly wanted to look at. Crumbling stone, cracked mortar, an ancient, dilapidated front door: the façade was as battered and weary as Ash felt. Ashland Park really took the *ancestral* in ancestral home to heart. All it wanted was the ghost of some disgruntled forebear to complete the scene, moans and footsteps, clanging chains at midnight.

With a sigh Ash turned, surveying the parkland which somehow managed to match the house's decrepitude, the lawn patchy, distant fences collapsing, a weedy stream of chimney smoke, as if the decay had seeped from the manor into the very soil and spread as far as the eye could see. It all served to emphasize just why he avoided coming home whenever he could.

He'd grown up in this house, he and Margaret and Mother. Father was often absent, and even his physical presence did not make much impact upon their daily lives. Father was persistently occupied, always too busy to have much to do with his offspring. Now, as an adult, Ash wondered what he'd been so busy with, as it certainly wasn't the restoration or management of the estate.

With his back thus to the door, he vowed he could feel the weight of it creeping onto his shoulders. The Ashland legacy, the name, the earldom, the future... All of it. He felt the ties to his heritage, felt an inkling of responsibility to the future, but had learned long ago not to invest too much of his heart or soul into anything related to this house. In honesty, he'd probably have sold it if it weren't entailed.

He'd been in a stupor for days. Wesley and the lads had seen to it, ensuring that his last moments of bachelorhood were well-spent in dissolution. He felt as if he'd been pickled in drink, desiccated and brittle. Standing at the front door of Ashland did not help matters.

And now he'd acquired himself a wife!

Ash had not wanted to marry Honora Botham. He hadn't, point of fact, wanted to marry anyone at all. Not at the moment. It was his opinion that a man ought not be leg shackled anywhere before the age of five and thirty, and having ten more years to that particular milestone, he could not help but feel cheated of a decade's worth of unencumbered living.

Moreover, this tradesman's offspring would most certainly not have been his choice of wife. In addition to her negligible pedigree, she was not at all physically suited to his womanly ideal. She was tall and thin, with no bosom to speak of, and shrewish. He was certain she was shrewish.

Had he been allowed the luxury of choice in the matter of his own mate, he might have picked someone like Lady Amelia Bates. Amelia was sweetly plump, round and soft in all the right places, and the top of her soft blond head came to just below his chin. This he knew from having danced with her on several occasions, occasions upon which he'd taken advantage of his lofty vantage point to stare down into her impressive décolletage. Amelia had quite the most generous bosom of any of the respectable girls of his acquaintance, round and high, and seemingly impossible for a gown to fully contain; they looked ever on the verge of popping out. Bounteous tits, Wesley'd called them.

Alas, Lady Amelia Bates' father was nearly as impoverished as Ash was himself, so it had never even been a consideration. Ash knew his duty to the family name. And he'd done it. Didn't mean he had to like it.

He stood on the threshold like this for some time, torn between entering and leaving.

Eventually the sun began to set and it became too dark to travel. He went inside.

* * *

"...twenty bedchambers; five drawing rooms; an orangery which has not been in use for seven years now; a portrait gallery; two overgrown formal gardens; a functional kitchen-garden; the library, the entire contents of which are entailed and thus significantly in need of conservation..."

Milton Perkins, the steward, went on and on as Honora's cheerless tour of Ashland Park continued. She followed him through the labyrinthine corridors, deprived of any and all sense of direction, unable to decide if the house itself or the list of repairs it required was more massive. There were empty rooms, and rooms full of moldering furniture, long hallways with tattered carpet, and empty places on the walls where paintings had once hung. In one section there were clear signs of water damage, heaps of damp plaster caved in from a hole in the ceiling. More than once Honora had held a handkerchief to her nose, blotting out stenches that shouldn't be found indoors. It was an entirely demoralizing experience.

Prudently, Honora had thoroughly investigated the entire Ashland family before committing herself to it, accessing information on its debts, investments, properties and any profligate spending habits. The ensuing generations had not been able to find their feet since the decline under the fifth earl, her husband's grandfather, the notorious gambler Lord Osmond Thorpe. Matters had deteriorated into ever more dire straits, year after year, until the lot of them were broke as beggars. Until now, of course, with the arrival of Honora, and all of her money.

Prepared as she thought she was, she could not deny a sense of shock at the extent of disrepair. And she had yet to peruse the household books.

Mr. Perkins had greeted her with the unabashed joy one usually reserved for the return of loved ones believed dead, and had wasted no time in propelling her throughout the house, listing everything that was wrong with the estate. She thought he'd expire with glee when she requested a detailed report of all the necessary repairs. Depressing, but the man was obviously not slacking in his duties, and Honora did prize enthusiasm.

Mr. Perkins finished his tour as Honora struggled to keep the dismay off her face. "A preliminary inspection, my lady. I hope to acquaint you with the issues confronting the estate in greater detail at your earliest convenience," he informed her, dashing any hopes that she'd seen the worst of it. Perkins bowed out of the room, leaving Honora in the study with a great pile of musty ledgers.

Honora plopped into a chair with a weary sigh, looking about the shabby room. Like everything else at Ashland Park, it was well past its glory days, neglected and unloved, rapidly descending from disrepair to outright disaster. At that moment, she acutely felt the weight of the task before her, the house, the estate and the family that came with it.

The situation was barely tolerable to the dowager countess, Lady Celeste. At their first meeting, her new mother-in-law had looked her up and down with the mixture of horror, fear and reluctant curiosity typically directed at large spiders. Overcome by the ten minute ordeal of speaking to her common daughter-in-law, Lady Celeste had quickly retired to her rooms to recuperate.

Then there had been a strained moment during the first family meal, when Lady Celeste had moved to her accustomed place at the foot of the table. Her eyes locked on Honora, who had moved to the chair as well. Honora held her glance with a small gracious smile, neither woman moving. It might not be easy for Lady Celeste to cede, but as the new countess, this was Honora's place, and she would take it. *Begin as you mean to go on*, Granny had always said, though the action would certainly do nothing to endear her to the dowager.

With a pained look at Ashland, who watched them silently from across the table, Lady Celeste finally moved to another seat.

That particular meal had proceeded in near silence, and Lady Celeste had at its completion yet again fled to her room.

The other member of the family, Ashland's sister Margaret, was amiable enough, and concerned primarily with her upcoming season. She was a fetching girl, resembling her brother without being as striking, and did not seem to have any particular aversion to Honora's presence in the house.

That morning, Honora had waited, assuming Ashland would accompany her on the survey of the house. After sitting for some time, she sent a servant to inquire as to his whereabouts, and was apprised that his lordship was still abed. Lady Celeste and Margaret, who had been seated with her, made no move to volunteer their company, and thus Honora had found herself the only participant of Mr. Perkin's dismal tour.

Thus far she had barely seen or spoken to Ashland. Perhaps he was avoiding her, or perhaps this was merely a typical aristocratic marriage. She had nothing to compare it to: Granny had already been a widow when Honora had gone to live with her after the death of her own parents. Still, she had imagined that Ashland would want to be involved in the restoration process at Ashland Park. She'd certainly assumed they would have more than passing interaction at meal times.

Nor had he made another attempt at claiming his husbandly rights. Honora had tried to put the disappointing wedding night out of her thoughts, hopeful that future nights would be more satisfactory, equally hopeful that one of those nights would come soon.

As she sat, idly toying with the cover of a ledger, she wondered at these people, the Thorpes of Ashland Park, who were so careless and thoughtless that they'd thrown away all they'd been given, and had never lifted a finger to put things right. Their biggest effort had been this, Ashland's marriage to her, and as far as she could tell, not a one of them intended to do a thing more. The actual work, the dirtying of hands, was evidently to be left to her mercantile abilities alone. It was a dispiriting realization.

* * *

A few days later, she was surprised to find the room already occupied by the dowager when she went down to breakfast. Lady Celeste had thus far been taking many meals in her room, and wasn't often without Margaret at her side.

"Good morning," Honora greeted her and took the chair beside her. She spread the napkin in her lap as a footman filled her plate.

"Good morning." Lady Celeste took a tiny bite of egg and dabbed delicately at her mouth.

"I trust you slept well?" Honora inquired in an inane attempt at politeness, as the footman placed her plate before her. She took a surreptitious breath, inhaling the smell of the hot, fragrant food, not wanting to confirm any of her mother-in-law's notions of her ill-breeding by a lascivious display of healthy appetite.

"Well enough." Lady Celeste took a slow, dainty sip of her tea. Honora could not help but feel that her each and every motion was halved: she took half a sip, half a bite and moved at half the speed. Although Honora hadn't noticed, she probably walked in tiny half-steps as well.

Just now a tiny, half-frown marred her elegant brow. "And how are you adapting? I daresay all this must be rather a change for you?"

"Indeed," Honora responded readily, thinking of the dilapidated state of her new home. Lady Celeste was probably referring to the historic and supposed majestic aspect of the place. While undeniably historic—the first stones of Ashland Park were laid some three hundred years ago—its current incarnation was a shadow of the stately home it had once been.

With a twinge of longing Honora thought of her own home in London, unabashedly new, vulgarly filled with every modern, new-moneyed convenience available. The windows weren't drafty, none of the linens smelled of mildew and there were few mysterious noises or odors. In London she had her own bathing room, with steaming hot water available at the twist of a tap. For her bath last night the Ashland servants had had to haul buckets of hot water up the stairs in a process that took nearly half an hour, by which point the water had cooled considerably.

"Of course," Lady Celeste continued, "Ashland Park has had its share of setbacks in these uncertain times, but I'm certain Ashland will take matters in hand now that… well." She trailed off, clearly unwilling to be so crass as to actually mention Honora's money, or the marriage itself. As for Ashland, the chances of him taking anything "in hand" seemed rather low. Thus far he had indulged mostly in an intense program of relaxation, with little evidence that the progress and development of the estate held any interest for him.

Honora made a vague sound and focused on her tea, and they ate in silence for a while.

"Margaret and I must go down to London soon. There is quite a lot to do, and I think it best we go as soon as possible," Lady Celeste said on a half-sigh, as though the task before her were dauntless, even though Honora could detect a tell-tale gleam of excitement in her eye.

"She will need all manner of things for her season," Lady Celeste continued, "and I do so want to take the time to have things properly made. This is a most important time for a gentlewoman. Her entire future is decided during her season, and we do so hope for a *proper* match."

"Of course," Honora answered, choosing to overlook the tone of the last comment, not sure if the dowager were being subversively snide, or if she herself were being particularly defensive. "The house is ready, and the servants will naturally be at your disposal."

"The house?" Lady Celeste looked at her, puzzled.

"My home, in London."

"Oh! No!" Lady Celeste half-laughed. "Oh, heavens my." She blotted her lips, eyes shining with what for her must be excessive mirth.

"We require accommodation that will reflect Margaret's status as the sister of an earl. Doubtless we will be receiving many callers, for I have a good deal of acquaintance in London that will wish to see me, and surely Margaret will have many new friends and suitors."

Honora strove to keep the edge out of her voice. "I assure you my home is sufficient to your needs –
"

"Doubtless it is sufficient to your needs," Lady Celeste patronized, "but there are so many requirements for a girl of Margaret's standing. One must consider the location, and furnishings, and of course the neighbors..."

She carried on, detailing the many necessities she assumed Honora's home would not be able to provide as Honora's breakfast grew cold on the table before her. It was insulting enough, but the way the woman assumed the money would simply pour forth was utterly galling.

"We have been so long away from London," Lady Celeste sighed, gazing longingly into the middle distance. "I will have Ashland write to the agent today."

Honora, out of patience and desperate to put an end to this ridiculous monologue, put down her fork and finally spoke. "Absolutely out of the question."

Lady Celeste finally turned to her and stared, her mouth hanging half-way open in a tiny 'O' of astonishment.

* * *

Ash stared out the window at a sliver of blue sky framed by the curtain's edge. There'd been a small white cloud in one corner which had disappeared a while ago. Occasionally a bird or two flew by, a dark blur of movement across the view, there and gone. He drummed his fingers lazily across his chest, envying them their freedom.

Damn, he wished Wesley were here. Devil knew he could use a good laugh, and if there were anything Wesley was consistently known for, it was a hell of a good time. He'd be the perfect antidote to his new wife's dreadfully earnest seriousness.

The new wife, as if summoned by his thoughts, suddenly appeared. The drawing room, where he'd gone to put his feet up and ponder his fate, suddenly shrank. She paused at the door in a swish of skirts, as though startled at the site of him, and there it was again, that perfectly awful little furrow of concentration between her brows. Zounds, but the woman was always frowning.

"Good day," she said, and resumed her entrance, taking a seat opposite him, smoothing her gown primly about herself. Ash swung his feet off the sofa and faced her, vaguely bothered by the idea that she had sought him out for some sort of conversation. But then a servant entered with tea, and he realized just how far gone the day was.

The wife silently focused on the servant and the tea, sparing him no look. He glanced at her once or twice, idly, wondering where his mother and sister had gone off to.

"Your mother and sister have gone to call at the vicarage," she said, uncannily guessing his thoughts as she handed him a cup of tea. She neatly assembled a small plate of sandwiches and biscuits, and handed that to him as well. "I was hoping we might have a moment to speak privately."

Of course she was.

He could only nod at her expectant expression. She brushed a speck of lint from her lap and glanced at him from beneath her lashes. He got the impression her eyes were a mere brown before she licked her lips, and diverted his attention. Her lips were rather satisfactory, he supposed, soft and pink, the bottom one particularly plump and just now dewy, a very nice contrast to her creamy skin.

"As you may be aware," she said, diverting his attention yet again, "I have been surveying the estate in an attempt to assess the magnitude of work which will be required..."

She continued on, but Ash's mind did the oddest thing upon hearing the words 'magnitude of work', and simply stopped listening. It was a bad habit of his, one which seemed to flare up with special intensity at most things involving the restoration of the family seat. Honestly, he wouldn't have gotten through any of the nuptial negotiations without the solicitor, and he'd really rather hoped that his new countess would use her not-insignificant business experience to handle matters. She ran a company, after all, and had all sorts of knowledge a man of his background did not.

She expelled a breath, closing her monologue, "...regarding Lady Ashland's desire to take a house in Town for the season."

To which Ash had no response. He didn't know what she was talking about. He took a sandwich. His wife folded in her lips.

"Allow me to be blunt, then. Your mother does not have the funds to take a house."

Ash stopped chewing. She stared steadily back at him.

"I'm sure I don't take your meaning," he said, putting down his plate, suddenly terrified that it had all been a horrific misunderstanding and she was not rich at all, that he had leg-shackled himself for no reason.

"They will stay at my home in Town. I've told her there is ample space, but she will not hear it."

"Why," he slowly began, "should she not take her own house if she wishes it, when she does now have the funds? Funds, of course, and your ample possession of such, being the entire reason for our recent nuptials."

There was a pause, for the space of a breath. "Did you not read the marriage settlement?"

He shot her a disagreeable look, and yes—there it was—the frown, pinched and deep between her brows.

"The Ashland family is penniless—"

"And that is no secret."

"Penniless," she continued, undeterred, "and virtually deplete of assets. You have nothing but that which is entailed, and the goal, obviously, in marrying me was to erase the family's debt and restore the Ashland standing and name. There is a business model and it was distinctly laid out in the settlement."

"I did my part, at the altar." He helped himself to another sandwich, though a significant lump seemed to be growing in his throat.

"There is more." She paused, worrying her lip. "The endeavor to restore the family's finances is complex and layered. It will take financial expertise and security, it will take a precious deal of time."

"Do kindly stop condescending to me and say what it is you need to say."

"*You* have no funds." She looked directly at him. "I retain all control over all my money."

* * *

"The devil you say!"

Oh, but he was furious. Absolutely pinch-faced and white-knuckled with rage. She fully expected him to break something, quite probably that crystal decanter on the sideboard, at any moment. Its sparkling facets seemed to call for a good smashing.

"It is clearly spelled out in the marriage agreement, my lord," Mr. Hamersley calmly repeated. Yes, the solicitors had been summoned, both her own and Mr. Hughes, the Ashland family representative, who sweated profusely under the earl's furious glare.

"Quite right, my lord, quite right," Mr. Hughes stammered. "The terms met with your approval. You did not contest them."

"We have the original documents bearing your signature and seal secured in our offices," Mr. Whitmarsh added. "Should you wish to re-read them." Whitmarsh was a consummate professional. Neither his features nor demeanor gave any indication of his true thoughts, but Honora had known him all of her life, and his disdain was writ clear.

Ashland flushed deep red and bit down on his cheek. It was painfully, bitterly obvious that he hadn't read the marriage agreement at all. Just as it was becoming painfully, bitterly obvious to Honora that she may have made a great error in judgement.

"You did not think to question this particular stipulation?" Ashland bit out, glaring at his attorney.

"I-it did seem unusual, my lord, but you did approve—" The look of fury on Ashland's face stopped him. Mr. Hughes drew a deep breath, and evidently some courage. "If I may be so bold, the arrangement—this marriage—is the salvation of this family. If the only way to do that was to allow Lady Ashland control over the finances, then so be it. She has demonstrated capability and responsibility in the management of her fortune, and I daresay she will do her utmost to restore the Ashland estate to what it once was."

Ashland turned his dark scowl to her. Honora raised her chin and stared right back. "Am I now to ask my wife for pocket money?" he asked in a low tone, not breaking eye contact, watching her with cold disdain.

The solicitors were silent. No one dared answer the question. Tension held the room, taught and steely. Honora bit down on her lip, schooling her tone and language to a calm she did not feel. "Absolutely not."

He raised a brow, somehow even in that simple gesture conveying the contempt he held for her.

"There is a budget allocated for your needs," she continued.

"By God, an *allowance*?" he bit out.

Honora was born of hard work, the same grit and determination that had raised her grandmother up from nothing to a respectable and successful life, the grandmother whose diligence had made her an heiress today. Honora was no fool. She knew how to manage her money. Since childhood she had been trained at her grandmother's hand to maintain and develop her finances, trained to advance the family's name and status. To this end, she always did, and would do, what needed to be done. She sat up straighter.

"If that is how you choose to think of it," she replied in altered tones, done trying to placate this man. She saw Messrs. Whitmarsh and Hamersley exchange a look. "You have a sufficient amount for your personal needs, clothing, clubs and whatnot, but any large purchases—any, in fact, decisions involving the expenditure of larger sums of money will be made by me. I retain sole control over all of my money, and will spend or invest as I deem best suited to the benefit and rejuvenation of the Ashland estate, and not to the whims, desires or fripperies of its members. Does that make it clear?"

Thick, heavy silence blanketed the room. If she'd been a man, the earl would certainly have hit her. She saw that there was no retreat from this moment. The stamp of revulsion and loathing in his eyes was indelible. Any look ever after would carry the trace of it, any hope of future regard would be built on the foundation of it.

No one spoke. She let the silence stretch and grow, and settle over her until it felt like the touch of a cold hand at the back of her neck.

CHAPTER FOUR

There were goddamn buggies and horses and workmen all over the house, all over the grounds, spilling and spreading like a contagion in close quarters, thought Ash. Every time he turned around there was someone in his way, *bettering* the goddamn estate.

It should please him, and the fact that it didn't only irritated him more. This was the care and attention that Ashland needed, this was why he'd married the heiress in the first place. Only instead of the relief and excitement he'd imagined feeling at this juncture, he felt like a spectator. The earl he might be, but there was no doubt that not a one of the workmen would take an order from him or give him more than a cursory nod and go about their business as prescribed by the squall of efficiency he'd married.

It was like she'd arrived at the estate with bricks and architect in tow, so quickly did the work commence. All of this chaos in a matter of weeks.

He ducked under the broad expanse of scaffolding and went into the house, where it was marginally quieter. The foyer was darker than usual, with most of the windows blocked by the work on the exterior, and Ash felt pierced anew by the gloom. Ashland at its best was a mildewed heap of old stones, one which he'd done a good job of tuning out, and he longed yet again for his humble bachelor's lodgings in London. He wanted his friends, Wesley and Cummings, he wanted back the unregulated days and nights of companionable dissipation that had defined his adult life thus far. Only now he'd done the right thing to restore a heritage he no longer had any control over. Most disheartening.

He went deeper into the house, suddenly famished for luncheon. He found his sister and wife in the dining room, and the meal just being served.

"Perfect timing as ever, Ash," Margaret exclaimed with a laugh. "Ride the morning away and waltz in at the moment the food touches the table."

Ash shot her a wry smile. "You're awfully cheerful."

"Honora and I were just discussing my wardrobe."

Ash glanced at his wife, who kept her gaze on her plate. "Oh?" he asked casually, as irritation rose in the back of his throat. "What's on the allowance, then? Two burlap gowns? Or perhaps we should see if anything's left in the attics from Grandmother's debut in '10?"

"Ashland!" Margaret scolded.

Honora only looked at him, a cool glance that gave nothing away. Indeed, he sincerely doubted she *had* anything to give away. Most likely her head was filled with mercantile concerns, long lists of accounts and expenditures, and had no room for the banalities of social intercourse.

"On the contrary," Margaret continued. "Honora has been recommending to me her own *modiste*, and we are to begin fittings as soon as we arrive in London."

He glanced again at his wife doubtfully. Her yellow gown was obviously of a good quality and masterfully made, but plain nonetheless, and free of virtually all adornment. Such was her entire persona. Her only jewels were tiny pearl earrings, the ring he'd presumably put on her finger at their wedding (he couldn't for the life of him recall), and a rather old and ugly necklace which was probably some family keepsake he was too infantile to understand.

She was not *bad* looking, he acknowledged to himself. She wore her thick, brown hair twisted up, although in not nearly as complicated a fashion as he'd seen on some ladies. Her neck, he could admit, was rather long and elegant, and the back of it looked remarkably soft and vulnerable. Her large brown eyes continually sparkled with intelligence and private humor, as though there were a joke only she understood. And her mouth. Well, her mouth was another matter, feminine, supple, like smooth pink velvet.

Ash forced his attentions back to his sister. He couldn't help a smile at Margaret's enthusiasm. The poor girl was getting a new lease on life, had up until now lived in diminished circumstances and limited prospects. She certainly deserved her fun. She was one of the biggest factors in his decision to marry now. Already nineteen, Margaret couldn't wait indefinitely for her season. God, but he hoped she'd make a marriage brilliant enough to justify his own.

With a start he realized that he had no idea what Margaret's dowry was. Certainly it had been mentioned, at some point, but the actual amount was a mystery. And though he was sure it would earn him another lecture, he requested to speak to his wife after luncheon.

"We must discuss the terms of Margaret's dowry," he began, as soon as his sister left the room. "She cannot be denied the opportunity to make the best possible match, or be rejected on the basis of an inadequate settlement." He turned, feeling more than a little heated at the notion of defending his sister's prospects. His wife sat at the table, watching him coolly. "The chief reason I married you at this point in time was to secure Margaret's dowry, and I will insist that she not be shortchanged, and provided with an amount reflective of her standing."

Honora waited a moment and spoke, "If you are finished…?" She rested both hands on the table and gave him the amount. "As you see, Margaret will be amply provided for. Furthermore, a portion remains set aside for her use exclusively. Her husband will be unable to touch it. I have high hopes for Margaret. She is an amiable girl, and she now has the means to be selective."

Ash made a small, non-committal sound. It was fair, more than fair, but perversely, he would not admit to as much. To do so would be an acknowledgement of her good decision, and he could not bring himself to it. She may have gotten this right, but she was still an over-reaching busybody.

"You are a paragon of efficiency." He made a mocking bow.

"Said with such derision. How, pray tell, does my competence offend you? You should—" she bit down on her lip, cutting herself off.

"I should…? What? Thank you?" He laughed harshly, feeling very far from amused. "I should, shouldn't I? And yet I won't."

* * *

When next she spotted Ashland, it was to see one of the workmen breaking his nose. Honora had been working, going over the incessant ledgers, until a growing disruption on the lawn drove her outdoors, along with a good number of the staff.

Ashland and the workman, who had the size and build of a sturdy house, stood across from one other, circling with their fists raised. Ashland, leanly muscled, perfectly proportioned, was puzzlingly and shockingly stripped to the waist. Honora had time to note the sheen of perspiration that coated his torso, when a large, beefy fist flashed from nowhere into Ashland's nose with a sickening crack, and blood exploded from his face.

A collective gasp went up from the assembled audience, which at that point included everyone from the upstairs scullery maid to the architect, and a majority of the workmen in between. As the blood erupted from the earl's nose, the scullery maid shrieked, the workmen scattered, and the architect stood by with a look of queasy shock. This Honora gathered in approximately one second, and then she was rushing to Ashland's side, where he'd landed splay-legged, hands clutching his face. He was already covered in blood. It poured freely from his nose, seeping out between his clenched fingers, coating his arms and chest.

As Honora knelt on the ground beside him, she cast another look at the spectators around them, and called out to one of the maids, "Run for towels, and have Hammond send for the doctor! And the constable! And you two," she yelled to a pair of footmen, "hold this man!" She jerked her chin to indicate the workman who'd done the damage.

The assailant yelled, "See here, now!", but the footmen did as she asked and quickly secured him, pinning his sizable arms behind him.

She then turned her attention back to the still profusely bleeding Ashland.

"Can you move your hands?" she asked, trying to get a better look at his injury. She touched the back of his hand, and he groaned. "Your nose must be broken. The doctor is on his way." She looked around the gathered group. There was still no sign of the maid with the towels. Spotting Ashland's discarded shirt nearby, she grabbed it.

"Move your hands," she said sternly as she grasped his wrists. His eyes, watching her above his clenched hands, looked at her as though she was insane. "I need to staunch the bleeding." She tugged his wrists, and he allowed it, wincing.

"S'not broken," he said, through a mouthful of blood.

Honora frowned, but bunched up his shirt and pressed it gingerly to his nostrils.

"Bloody hell!" Ash yelled.

"It's broken," she replied.

Hammond had clearly been made aware of the goings-on, for he was racing down the lawn with several sturdy footmen in his wake. The maid jogged along not too far behind, a mountain of white linens in her arms.

Then they were there, and she directed them to carry the earl to his rooms, after swathing most of his face and upper body in towels which quickly turned from white to red as the blood continued to pour out his nose. He seemed to be feeling the effects, for his head bobbed drunkenly as the footmen lifted him in a bier of their arms, and he made only weak protests, though the pain must have been enormous.

Honora watched as they carried him up the lawn with ginger steps, a thousand thoughts going through her head as the insanity of the past few minutes sank in. She doubted he'd bleed to death. He appeared far too hale and stubborn for something so trivial.

She looked around at the green grass, the blue sky, the stone of the manor glowing gold in the afternoon light. Such a pretty, normal place, and yet his lordship resorted to fisticuffs with a laborer.

She could see Hammond and her maid Poppy coming back out of the house. As they approached she could see Hammond holding something in his hands, a vial, no doubt of *sal ammoniac* to restore her shattered nerves.

Poppy gasped as she reached her, giving her a look of a horror as she took her in from head to toe. "My lady, you are covered in blood! Are you hurt?"

Honora glanced down. The front of her pale yellow gown was splotched with blood, and her knees were soaked in it from kneeling next to Ashland. Blood smeared her hands and wrists, and was already beginning to dry, turning from bright red to rusty brown. She grabbed a towel from Poppy and scrubbed her hands. "I daresay I look like I've been butchering hogs."

Poppy looked dismayed. Hammond carefully extended the *sal ammoniac* to her, plainly thinking she might be deranged from the shock. "There's no need for that, I assure you. It's not my blood. Has the workman been detained?"

"Yes, my lady." He nodded stiffly, his expression unchanged.

"I will go to his lordship. Call me when the constable arrives."

She marched off back towards the house, past a cluster of gawping servants. Ashland was in his bed, a bevy of maids and footman hovering in the room and outside the door. She dismissed them all, and entered her husband's bedchamber for the first time.

The room was enormous, done up in shades of long-faded blue, filled with furniture both old and large, ornate antiques befitting the ancient lineage of the family Ashland. Sunlight streamed in through large windows, illuminating the threadbare carpet.

He lay atop the coverlet, holding a bloody towel to his nose. On the floor beside his bed was a pile of blood-stained cloths. He looked up at her as she walked toward the bed, a doleful glance with more than a note of suspicion.

"It seems as though you've blackened both eyes, in addition to breaking your nose," she said. The skin under his eyes, that she could see, was already beginning to swell and turn blue.

"*I* didn't blacken them," he said stiffly.

"What were you doing fighting the workman?"

He clicked his tongue. "I was boxing, not fighting."

She raised a brow, seeing no difference.

"Boxing is a sport. There are rules. There is an elegance to it. It's a perfectly respectable way for gentlemen to discharge excessive energy."

"I don't think your opponent knew the rules," Honora said. Boxing, fighting, it all sounded idiotic to her. What's more, she was surprised to be unaware of this proclivity. Her future husband had been most thoroughly investigated during the betrothal negotiations, and she thought she'd known the full scope of his interests and activities, but she'd never heard of him boxing. "I suppose we can call off the constable."

"How is it that you are so comfortable around blood?" He indicated her bloody clothes with his chin. "This obviously is not your first time dealing with an injury."

"What makes you say so?"

"Someone was screeching, and even through the blinding pain, I could tell it wasn't you. You're the only one who kept her head out there."

"To be fair, I'm sure none of the staff are used to seeing their master engage in such a display of... boxing."

Honora tilted her head, looking down at the coverlet. She wondered how much to tell him, and realized it didn't matter at this point. She wasn't going to win him over, they were already married, and she doubted anything she revealed would make him dislike or resent her more.

"As part of my training—"

"Training?" he interrupted.

"Training to manage the family enterprises. I frequently accompanied my grandmother to visit the factories and mines."

"Your *grandmother* took you to *factories* and *mines*?" he asked, incredulous.

She had thought him odd for brawling on the lawn. The feeling was reciprocated; he obviously thought her education beyond peculiar. "My grandmother believed that a thorough access and knowledge of every aspect of the business was essential to successfully manage it. So, yes, I visited the factories, as well as the mines. The nature of the work was often dangerous, and there were injuries. It was dealt with."

"By you?"

"Granny didn't shy away from direct experience. Truthfully, it was beneficial. It taught me to keep a cool head under pressure, and as Granny always said, not too think too highly of myself, or that I was above getting my hands dirty."

Ash considered this for a moment. "Damned if I can argue with it. Though I'd never think it a suitable place for a female."

Honora felt the barb. She glanced away, unwilling for him to see any emotion on her face.

Ash moaned, and spit some blood into the towel. "Damn me if I'm not bleeding to death."

"Unlikely," Honora answered. "A broken nose looks worse than it is."

"Easy for you to say," he snapped.

Honora bit down on the corner of her lip. "You'd better worry the doctor can set it right. One wrong twist and you won't be so pretty anymore," she said archly.

He surprised her by laughing. The short guffaw was immediately followed by a wince, as the motion jarred his injured nose.

The doctor arrived and set Ash's nose, a quick procedure that involved a lot of loud cursing. The doctor's unsympathetic departing advice, "The mind of him who has understanding seeks knowledge, but the mouths of fools feed on folly," was likewise met with a comparably impolite response, and the recommendation of laudanum duly ignored in favor of brandy. The dowager, overcome by the day's ordeal, retreated to recover in her room, demanding the consoling company of her daughter, thereby conveniently continuing her strategy to ignore Honora whenever possible.

Thus Honora found herself dining alone in her room, pondering the state of her new life among a family that, with the exception of Margaret, openly disliked her. And the earl himself, stripped down and fighting on the lawn like a common drunkard, his blood as red as any other man's.

* * *

Some nights later there came a sound at her door, more of a bang than a knock that startled her out of her usual evening quiet. Puzzled, she opened it, half expecting to see a clumsy maid, but instead she found Ashland leaning against the doorframe. He'd donned a shirt, a large white billowy thing, untucked and disheveled as the rest of him. His hair stood on end, and a miasma of brandy surrounded him. He healed rapidly: his nose had mostly returned to its regular shape and the bruises under his eyes all but faded. Instead of bloody and pummeled he now managed to look rakishly appealing.

"You are vastly improved," Honora said.

He drew back, his head wobbly. "My face still hurts. Unbar the way and let me in." He pushed past her and went into the room.

"What," she asked, hand still on the open door, "are you doing?"

"Good God! Is that your nightdress?" He looked her up and down, obviously finding her serviceable linen wanting, and something inside Honora shifted. She recalled another nightdress, silk instead of linen, and not nearly so modest. She recalled the one night she'd worn it, never imagining he wouldn't notice it at all. The morning after her wedding night, she'd stuffed that Italian negligee under the mattress at the inn and left it there.

"Get out!"

"Don't yell," he winced.

"Don't sit down!" He plopped down into a chair before the unlit hearth.

"Good. God. I'd be remiss not to tell you that you are barking." He scowled at her.

"I'd be remiss not to tell you that you're a drunken boor," Honora replied, certain that she'd never spoken to anyone, ever, so harshly in all of her life. "And that you should leave at once." She gestured to the open door, but he would not budge.

"I believe it is time that we discussed some matters." He sank deeper into the chair, one long leg extended before him, the other bent at the knee. Honora saw with a small shock that he was barefoot. She'd never seen a man's bare feet before. It was oddly intimate, that.

The top few buttons of his shirt were undone, leaving it hanging open to reveal a deep amount of his chest. Honora swallowed. Being boorish, drunken and even bruised may have diminished his fine looks, but evidently did little to diminish Honora's persistent attraction to him.

She shut the door. Walked to the window. Then the desk. Then finally took a seat opposite her husband, folded her hands stiffly in her lap and looked up at him with her best effort at polite disinterest.

"The past few days have been rather enlightening. To put it mildly." He crossed his hands over his abdomen. "I think you can agree that these recent revelations, both to myself and my mother, have been upsetting. Not least of which is my own stupidity at failing to review the marriage contracts."

Honora did not argue. Failing to read a contract *was* the height of stupidity. Granny would roll in her grave if Honora ever made such a careless mistake.

"It was unwise on my part," he continued. "I just never imagined..." He trailed off, staring at his feet. Honora followed his gaze. Heavens, even his feet were finely made; long, gracefully arched, decidedly male with a sprinkling of hair.

Honora looked up. "You never imagined a wife would assume control?" she finished for him. She knew that's what he was getting at.

He lifted one shoulder. "Something like that."

"Be assured that I work in the best interests of the estate and the Ashland name. The situation is not irreparable and with attentiveness, it can be brought round. Though you may not feel it, I am now a member of this family, and my interests are inseparable from the interests of the estate. Indeed, what I build now is for the benefit of our future children."

Honora stopped, blushing so hard that a prickle of sweat broke out on her upper lip. Children! The very idea called to mind their begetting, and it was as though she'd asked him to get into bed right now. She stared down at his feet and blew out a surreptitious breath.

"It is better, after all," she continued, trying to regain some control. "I have the experience and diligence to set things right."

"There!" he said, and she looked up. "That's it. Do you have to be so bloody high-handed about it?"

"I beg your pardon!"

"The way you speak to me. The way you spoke to my mother. I'll allow that she might not need her own house in town, but did you have to be so autocratic about it? You might have explained it to her in gentler terms, instead of dismissing her request out of hand."

Honora frowned.

"We might not be the best managers of the estate and all it entails, but we're not children, either."

"I never—"

"Oh, yes. Yes, indeed you have. And you do treat us like irascible children, as though it's up to you to stop us from having too much cake and getting a belly ache."

"It might escape you that someone has to exercise a modicum of control, lest you all end up where you started!"

"Perhaps," he agreed, to her astonishment. "But I am the earl."

"In name only."

He stiffened all over, and though he didn't shift position, anger radiated from him.

"Do you realize," Honora continued calmly, "how hard people in your position work? The ones that want to retain their land and properties, and not squander it away on horses or drink or whatever other nonsense they feel themselves entitled to? I'd wager Swanson or Eldridge are out on the land daily, and they know their business."

Ash stared hard at her, his mouth a taut line, his eyes flinty. She'd probably—undoubtedly—gone too far in comparing him to Swanson and Eldridge, two of the nobility's more successful examples.

"You should have married one of them," he said flatly.

And Honora responded, "I might have done, were they not each already married."

Ashland's look went from outrage to aversion at her blunt agreement. "Alas, a wealthy man wouldn't need to sell his title to a rich bride. It is only those less prosperous among us who must do so."

It was all true, of course, but the subjective part of Honora's brain couldn't reconcile itself to the insult in his tone. *Never give credence to deprecation*, Granny would say. To acknowledge a thing was to make it stronger.

"We both of us know why we made this marriage," she said stiffly, tired of the Earl of Ashland and his conversation. She looked down and tried to dislike his ridiculously attractive feet.

"Nevertheless," he said after a while, with a new conciliatory tone. He paused until she looked up at his face. His expression changed. He watched her with a half-smile, a gleam in his eye. Even battered and bruised he was utterly appealing, perhaps even more so, stripped away of any semblance of polish and veneer, rough and completely, unapologetically male.

"Nevertheless," he began again with a knowing look that sent a lick of heat through her, "we are surely both creatures of sense, capable of reason and discourse, of communicating with one another in a fashion that will ensure our mutual satisfaction in the years to come. We have hardly begun to experience married life. Not properly, as a man and woman."

He shifted in his chair, one motion concentrated in the hips. Honora's breathing faltered.

She realized that he was attempting to seduce her, all heavy-lidded and suggestive and potent. *Why?* She wondered. Did he hope to achieve some sort of advantage? Some sort of concession on her part, or was seduction the goal in and of itself?

She might be outraged. Only, she didn't mind so much. As long as she was clear on his motives, however clever he might think himself. They were married, after all, and one did want to experience *that* part of marriage. She watched him evenly, her blood beginning to spark.

"What are contracts and solicitors between two people?" he said in a low voice that sent a shiver up her spine. "As man and wife, shouldn't we be able to reach an agreement on our own terms, as benefits us as individuals and not as figures on a piece of parchment? We spend our days arguing, working. Surely there is more to marriage."

"Surely," she agreed, her mouth suddenly dry. One of his brows went up. He took her meaning completely. The atmosphere in the room changed abruptly. She licked her lips.

He stood up, not taking his eyes from her. Honora stood as well, and in a few steps he was before her, radiating heat and masculine intent, and the lingering aroma of brandy.

There was nothing beneath her nightgown. Only a thin layer of linen separated her skin from his. Thus when he reached around and cupped her buttocks, she inhaled sharply, for the warmth of his palms went immediately through to her bare skin. He pulled her toward him, her hands going uncertainly to his chest.

He exhaled against her temple with a small sound, and brought her closer, lifting her as he arched against her. She felt him pressed clearly against her, his manhood, his *cock,* hard and insistent, and desire broke through her in a liquid wave. It burned low in her belly, and there, in the needy spot between her legs where he rubbed against her.

So she did what she had long wanted to: reached up to kiss the spot beneath his jaw. Here the scent was intensely male, intensely him, and she took the tiniest taste, the tip of her tongue finding the heady sweet-salty mixture of his skin.

He moved her toward the bed, rucking up her gown along the way. They toppled backward, a fall of limbs and tangled bedclothes. As Honora shifted up the bed, head swimming, Ash reached down to undo his buttons, and she had only a glimpse of that mysterious male part before it was between her legs, and abruptly inside her.

For a moment he paused, held still on his arms above her, and Honora arched against him as the pleasure stretched and grew. It centered there, at their connection, and spread throughout her belly, to the hard tips of her breasts, to the breath that had become a shallow panting. She put her hands against his shoulders, wanting to feel him everywhere.

He began to move then, in a fast rhythm, his eyes open and focused on the headboard. Honora shifted a bit against the rapid thrusting. Her hips were lodged in an awkward position, but his weight prevented her movement. A touch of discomfort intruded on the pleasure, and she wanted him to pause so that she might readjust her position, but it did not seem a request one ought to voice at such a moment.

She wanted…something, something elusive as the intensity of the moment diminished. She wanted the sensations of a moment ago back, but they edged away, replaced by a nameless frustration as he kept on moving above her, inside her but somehow apart from her, and she felt herself coldly separated from the act.

He kept on at the same quick tempo, moving and staring ahead, until he stopped suddenly, wracked by a shudder that annoyed her. It wasn't until he moved off of her a minute later that she understood it was all over. She lay there, wilted and confused, wondering what had gone so wrong, wanting nothing so much as to pummel something.

CHAPTER FIVE

In due course Margaret and the Dowager prepared to depart for London. Lady Celeste comported herself as one bound for incarceration, and not for what was likely one of the most modern, well-appointed homes in Town. Honora did not bother correcting her. After her initial failed attempt at describing her home, she'd let her mother-in-law wallow in her misconceptions as a fit chastisement for her rudeness. She tried to encourage Margaret, who was so sweetly enthusiastic about her debut and London and new gowns that Honora couldn't help but feel the slightest bit envious at the girl's excitement. What Honora had to look forward to was more ledgers and fund reallocations and meetings. She would also, for the first time since they'd married, be alone in the house with Ashland.

Honora stood in the foyer with Margaret as the baggage was assembled, while Lady Celeste flitted in and out, issuing orders and complaints as they occurred to her.

"Put it over there," she commanded two footmen balancing a large trunk, and then seemingly still addressing those same two footmen, "Oh, when I think of my father's townhouse, and the elegant parties, and all the finest callers my mother so proudly received."

The bemused footman watched her, thumping down the trunk. "Careful, careful! I suppose I shall make do with receiving very few callers, or seeing many of my old friends…" She continued on in this vein, going back upstairs to oversee her maid.

Honora bit her lip, fighting the urge to laugh and roll her eyes at the same time. Surely Lady Celeste had been confined to Ashland Park for too long, and thus elevated it to a status it had long ceased to possess. It might still carry the weight of the ancient Ashland name, but leaking ceilings, crumbling mortar and drafty halls had stripped it of any of its former elegance. Lady Celeste could not see it for what it was: a rotting behemoth, sucking away far too much time and money.

Though it had come a small way with the improvements of the last few weeks, it had so much further to go, and Honora would need to return to London soon to oversee her other business concerns. The vague hope that her husband might overtake some of the estate's management had faded, and thus she would need to take the time to convey explicit instructions to Perkins.

The lord of the manor himself entered the foyer, looking about at the mountains of trunks and cases.

"I thought you were buying all new things?" he asked, raising a brow at his sister.

"Oh, don't tease," Margaret huffed. "You know Mother can't leave a thing behind." This was obviously true, as Lady Celeste appeared at the top of the stairs with a trail of baggage-laden maids and footmen behind her. Margaret moved aside to confer with her maid, leaving Honora standing alone with Ashland. He slanted her a look, but didn't speak. Honora supposed he was still perturbed over the failed results of his seduction, their last connubial encounter having concluded in an awkward parting and not the loss of her senses that he'd seemed to expect.

She herself had been experiencing a vague antipathy towards him since that evening and avoided meeting his eye.

Eventually, with warm hugs and good wishes for Ashland, and a cooler farewell to Honora, the ladies were off. Honora stood with Ashland on the stairs with a handful of servants, waving until the carriages disappeared down the drive. It was a fine day for travel, sunny and dry. Their journey should be an easy one. The physical one, at least. The

Dowager's emotional journey to her newly-martyred status would likely be a bit more trying.

They all lingered for a minute, taking a moment to enjoy the sunshine and fresh air, and then the group dispersed, the servants to their work, Honora to hers, and Ashland to whatever leisurely pursuit he had assigned himself for the day.

Honora remained closeted in the study throughout the remainder of the day, powering through the ledgers and finalizing a budget for the Ashland Park renovations, as well as attending to a packet from London requiring her attention on some other business holdings. It was unusually quiet. Lady Celeste and Margaret hadn't been a particularly loud or engaging presence, yet their absence echoed throughout the house. She worked until afternoon, and then deciding she'd had enough with being stifled indoors, headed outside for a walk to clear her head.

It was lovely out of doors. While the grounds needed their fair share of work, they were perfection compared to the house, and Honora decided to walk as far as she could under the blue sky.

The gardens had gone to ruin. One could see that they'd once existed, beyond that, there was no evidence of their previous beauty. There was still a functioning kitchen garden, and a small plot of flowers, a meager medley of early blooms, cultivated by the dowager or Margaret, she did not know, that looked like they were losing the battle to survive.

The parkland, as a more natural landscape, was still beautiful, extending in green waves in every direction. The sun shone pleasantly, the clean air proved a refreshing tonic, and she was altogether glad she'd come outside.

As she walked, she thought of the changes of the past few weeks, and the unexpected direction her marriage had taken.

She hadn't expected Ashland to fall at her feet and declare his love. She was an individual blessed with a remarkable degree of practicality. What she could not deny, at least to herself, was the secret desire she'd nourished for friendship and companionship in matrimony. She'd envisioned them working together to rebuild, developing a partnership of sorts if nothing else.

What troubled her most was not so much his disdain, though that in itself was far from ideal, but his utter indifference to the situation before them. The title, the house, the name, all were his, and he exhibited not the least regard for any of it.

Her error was in assumption: She had assumed a common goal would unite them. Instead it seemed clear she was to have none of the comforts of marriage, neither the friend nor the sporting bedmate. The realization did not sit well.

After some time she spotted a group of people in the distance, what looked like several men. As she approached, she saw three of them were farmers and the other was Ashland, and they appeared to be focused on repairing a fence. To her amazement, Ashland was in his shirtsleeves, doing the brunt of the work.

One of the men spotted her, and gave a wave. Honora waved back, pleased to be greeted so enthusiastically. The man gave a shout, and Ashland's head lifted, taking in her approach. He, too, said something, but the words were lost over the distance. Honora hastened to approach through the grass, wondering what they wanted to tell her. Another farmer separated from the group, and began making his way towards her, again shouting out a message that she couldn't make out.

She understood in a few more steps, as her foot landed in something warm and altogether foul. She didn't need to look down to know she'd step right into a fresh cow patty, the stench was enough to alert her.

The farmer finally caught up to her, saying, "T'is a cow pasture, my lady. Watch your step."

"I'm afraid it's a bit too late," she said stiffly. She'd left the house on impulse, and hadn't thought to change into walking shoes. Her slippers had seemed adequate to the dry terrain, but they were definitely inadequate to stepping into a large pile of bovine feces, offering no protection to her stockinged foot.

To his credit, the man did not laugh. He merely extended her an arm and escorted her to the others at the fence, and Honora squished silently along, holding her hem high.

The same could not be said for Ashland. He glanced at her over the fence, took in her expression and said, "You didn't."

"Oh," she replied with a shudder, "I most emphatically did. My slipper is ruined." She extended her foot to prove her point.

He glanced down at her shoe and then back up at her face, a twitch at the corner of his mouth. "Well, shit."

One of the other men burst out laughing, then quickly covered it with a cough, turning away with a mortified look at Honora. Her husband spared no such kindness. He laughed deeply and openly. The farmers tried for politeness, but the humor of the situation won out until they were laughing as well. Honora supposed it was somewhat amusing, but the rapidly cooling matter on her foot dampened her mirth.

"Did you not hear us warning you to watch your step?" Ashland asked after a minute.

She shot him a look in response.

Still chuckling, he bid the farmers goodbye, arranging to meet them the next day at another section of fencing. They gathered their supplies and headed off across the fields, no doubt skillfully avoiding any unpleasant surprises.

Ashland turned to Honora, taking in her one-legged pose. He knelt down before her, asking,

"May I?" With a deft movement his hands went under her gown and fastened around her leg.

"Eep!"

"Don't squirm," he said into her skirts, and began unfastening her garter. He rolled down her stocking, and wedged it down over her slipper, managing to get the whole filthy lot down in one. When he flung the entire thing into the field, Honora could not help but laugh. She wiped her foot along the grass, and then wiggled her bare toes at the odd sensation.

"You can ride Alfred back. If you can manage astride?" he asked, lifting one brow.

"Of course," Honora replied with more surety than she felt, never before having ridden astride.

Ashland had a charming quirk, in that one corner of his mouth—the left—had to it a natural curve, giving him a perpetual expression of natural amusement, as though a private joke hid just there, and if you were fortunate, you might be made privy to it. That was the look he gave her now, before turning away to collect his coat and few other belongings scattered around the fence. Honora swallowed thickly, feeling of a sudden extra warm.

"Is something amiss with the fencing?" she asked, mostly to introduce a new subject.

"Just normal repairs. Nothing out of the ordinary."

"We could send someone into the fields."

Ash shook his head but did not answer. Gathering the rest of his things, he took the horse's reins and led it over to Honora. The horse was an enormous, implacable-eyed thing, and with a few movements, Ashland had her foot in his clasped hands and was hoisting her onto its back. It was beyond odd to shift her right leg across the saddle, her skirts billowing up and around her, and she held tight, feeling for a moment as if she might topple over. She gave Alfred a pat, assuring him of her friendly intentions.

It was a bit awkward, no less so for the way her gown hiked up and exposed her legs from the calf down, one stockinged, one bare. There was little to be done for it, so she shook the discomfort off. It was unlikely anyone would be about, and certainly her husband didn't seem to care a farthing about her naked limbs.

Ashland took the lead, and they began making their way back to the house. The sun shone brilliantly overhead, while a gentle breeze washed over the landscape. The air was sweet and pure, though the odor of dung lingered in Honora's nostrils.

"I was a lad with these men," Ashland said, and she realized he was addressing her question about the fence. "We used to roam these fields and the woods and everything in between. Then I went away to school, became the lord while they became farmers. When I'm home, I sometimes come out in the guise of lordly benevolence, and they let me, and we get a few things done. I can't very well invite them to tea. And out here, in the fields, they see me more as the boy they remember, and they're freer with their words. It's the only way I can ever figure out what's happening with the tenants."

He had a warmth about him, obviously content in the moments of camaraderie he'd spent with his former friends, and likely from the fresh air and sunshine. Honora felt it herself. Despite her bare foot and the accident that had caused it, it was wonderful being outside. She wiggled her bare toes in the stirrup.

"Why did you come out?" Ashland asked. "Did you need me for something?"

"I needed a break from the accounts. My head was fair swimming."

He made a small sound of amusement. "Next time you might consider sturdier footwear."

"I might," she replied with no ire. After all, it hadn't been the wisest thing to hike into the countryside in nothing but a pair of dainty slippers.

"And how are the accounts faring these days?" He looked into the distance as he asked, his tone casual, though she sensed his interest was anything but.

"As dismal as ever," she sunnily replied, earning herself a sharp look. She laughed. "Matters cannot be turned around so quickly. Even by me."

"You certainly spared no time in getting the repairs to the house started," he pointed out.

"Bricks and mortar aren't difficult to repair, all it needs is hands. A team of men, an architect and some time, and Ashland Park will be restored. The finances, on the other hand, are a more complicated beast. I need to go over the accounts as far back as I can, and work from there. There are debts, and investments, and future budgets—"

He raised a hand, and tossed her a look over his shoulder, clearly begging for mercy. "I would rather restore every fence in England. Single-handedly."

Honora did not doubt it. It wasn't as though he'd ever even pretended to be interested in these matters.

That was wrong, she realized with a jolt. She's just seen the first real evidence of his concern, working with the farmers on the fence. He obviously had a care for the men, his own tenants, and he'd been working on things with his own hands. Honora began to feel the first inklings of hope. Perhaps his strength was not in accounts and ledgers, but in the physical state of things. He was an active, outdoorsy type of man, as evidenced by his lean muscular build. Perhaps his abilities would best be directed at that aspect of things.

"Yes, well, it's not my favorite either, you know," she said. He gave her another look over his shoulder. "You needn't look so incredulous. Accounts are dull and tedious and a lot of hard work, but Granny—"

"Ah, yes, the inimitable Granny," he added dryly.

"Inimitable indeed," Honora replied stiffly.

"Oh, come now." Ashland sighed, giving the lead a little swing. "Don't be offended. It's only Granny seemed to have given a lot of advice."

"She did, and I would be a fool not to follow it. My grandmother was a wise woman, more intelligent than any man I've ever known, and she had a fine head for business. She was the force behind Botham industries." The nerve of the man!

"And what of Grandfather Botham? Or your father?"

"They both led unfortunately short lives."

"So it was Granny Botham who raised you?"

Honora huffed in irritation, and he turned to look at her in bewilderment, slowing the horse. "Don't you know anything about me? Didn't you learn anything at all before we wed?"

That corner of his mouth quirked up in devilish amusement. "I know you're rich."

Honora tore her gaze from his, looking off into the distance, the hills and trees and everything as far as she could see Ashland land. "You are as terrible at matrimony as you are at business."

He made a sound, like an offended laugh, but Honora did not care. "I know your grandfather bankrupted the family with his gambling."

"As does everyone," he said icily.

Honora looked down at him. "I know your father died when you were seventeen, and that you were called down from school to come home and run the estate. I know you sold anything that your father hadn't."

One brow raised in response, daring her to go on.

"I know the bachelor rooms in which you live, the clubs you frequent, the debts you owe. I know you!"

He stopped suddenly, turning on one heel to pierce her with an irate look. Honora tilted in the saddle. She tightened her hold on the reins as he stepped toward her. And when he rested his hand on her bare leg, she almost jumped out of her seat.

"Don't be absurd! You've done your research, I'll grant you that, but don't assume that makes you know me. Even I, Honora, am more than the sum of my parts."

It was the very first time he'd ever said her name—a part of her was somewhat surprised he even knew it—and it had come out with such scorn. Honora sighed wearily.

His hand wrapped around her exposed calf and Honora wasn't altogether certain he wasn't about to shove her off the mount. Heat spread from the place he touched her, even as he scolded her. Honora wanted to look away from his irate gaze, but did not, held it steady, certain her cheeks were glowing bright red.

"I am not my father, nor my grandfather. They destroyed the estate; I am saving it."

Honora wanted to retort that she was the one doing the saving, but held her tongue. No easy feat, as she was not typically given to restraint. Standing there as the breeze picked up, he looked like nothing so much as a country squire, tousle-haired, shirt billowing in the wind and mud on his sturdy boots. She thought of him working on the fence, and said nothing.

After a long moment he spoke again, not turning to look at her. "Pray tell me, did you unearth any other enlightening facts about the Ashland family? Our impecunious state was well-known. We were forthright about that. What else, exactly, were you hoping to discover?"

"You've no need to take offense."

"I assure you I do not."

"I would never enter any business arrangement blindly."

"Business arrangement?" This did bring his head around. He stared at her in distaste.

She raised a brow. "Surely we can speak openly. We're neither of us here for anything else. You yourself have commented on my detached commercial heart." Ignoring his sound of token disagreement, she continued, "At the least we have no need of pretense. We have that between us."

"Cold-blooded honesty?"

"Yes."

"You are a singular creature."

"I am what I am, and I daresay you should be grateful for it." He frowned, puzzled. "I am not some empty-headed chit, with a full purse and no sense. Money alone will not help Ashland. Restoration requires a sure hand, planning and determination. Think what you will of me, but I know what I'm doing. And I would be a fool to enter into a marriage unprepared. So, yes, I did my research, and studied you all."

They continued on. He did not look at her. She could see from the rigid set of his shoulders and his tight hold on the reins that he was not pleased, but then, it was unlikely that he would ever be pleased with her, so she'd best let go the notion.

"And?" he asked.

Honora stared at the back of his head in confusion.

"What did your enquiries reveal about the once-vaunted Ashland family? If you tell me there's a madwoman in the attic I might just board the next ship for America."

Honora could not help a small smile despite herself. "Nothing of the sort, becalm yourself. The greatest fault in your family appears to be poor judgment and lavish spending. There's the odd scandal, Mrs. Goodson and the children, of course, a duel or two a generation past." Honora looked out over the lush green scenery, promising herself that she would take a full tour of the parklands at the first opportunity. Surely there was more to enjoy at the estate than pouring over musty ledgers. Why, the countryside here was breathtaking.

"Mrs. Goodson?"

Engrossed in the lush landscape, Honora answered without thinking, "Your father's mistress and their children."

The horse snickered in protest when Ash suddenly stopped again, jerking on the reins as he spun around, ripping her focus from her surroundings.

"Is this your idea of a joke?" From the look on his face it was patently clear he had not known about Mrs. Goodson, or the children. He stared up at her, anger and bewilderment playing across his features. Something in Honora's stomach plummeted, a flip-flop spin of mortification that she might have just blurted out information he had not been familiar with.

"Of course not!" Honora gasped, mind scrambling how best to assuage the situation. "I assumed you knew!" His mouth pressed into a taut line, his lips paling against his skin, disconcerting Honora. She would never have spoken of it had she suspected that he was ignorant of the matter. Frowning and stormy-eyed, there was more emotion in his face than she'd ever glimpsed before. Guilt churned along with the mortification in her belly. She pushed a hand against her navel, pressing it down.

"It wasn't precisely the best-kept secret," she soothed, hoping she didn't sound as defensive as she felt. "The woman lives not seven miles from here. My agents discovered her existence in the most perfunctory fashion."

He looked away and swore. "Seven miles?"

Honora remained silent, feeling she'd delivered enough of a shock for one conversation, and perhaps too many particulars.

Ashland's expression grew drastically darker when he turned back to her. "You know where she is? You will provide me with her direction. No," he preempted when she opened her mouth to protest. "You will do this."

"But what will you do? What are you hoping to gain?" Honora began to feel a sense of concern for the unknown mistress. Would he in his shock and anger lay the blame of the relationship at her feet, try to deliver some punishment?

He ignored her questions. "What else do you know about them?"

"Nothing, really. I have a file in London—"

"Of course."

Honora bit back a retort, urging herself to understand his current state of mind.

"Like it or not," he said eventually, "you are the one who has delivered this news and you must bear some of the consequences."

Bearing the consequences for this family's bad decisions seemed to be her new role in life. Still, it wasn't information that could be kept secret. He could simply find the information elsewhere, and delaying him would likely only alienate him more.

"Alright," she conceded, "but I'm going with you." He didn't look too happy at the prospect, but Honora held his eye, not backing down, until he gave her a curt nod. And she did feel a sense of responsibility for this latest uproar, both to him and to this unknown woman upon whom he would descend and unleash who knew what matter of mayhem. At the very least, her presence might inject a measure of civility and keep matters from getting out of hand. Or so she hoped.

They continued on. After a while she said to his back, "I truly really didn't realize you didn't know about them." He said nothing, gave no indication that he'd heard her. He led the rest of the way in silence, helping her dismount at the front of the house. As soon as her feet touched the ground, he was in the saddle, and without a word turned and rode off across the park.

* * *

"Rutting old bastard." Ash cursed his father, wondering for the hundredth time since he'd learned the news of his pater's second family how a man who'd never shown any interest in his two legitimate children could be bothered to create more on the side. Under their very noses, no less. And to not have known! He must be the laughingstock of all Leicestershire.

"Do you think my mother knows?" he asked his wife. He could see her in his peripheral vision, keeping a wary eye on him. She had not been supportive of his plan to visit Mrs. Goodson, and only insisted on accompanying him to keep him calm. A fairly strong rain had spoiled his original plan to ride out on horseback, thus he and the ever estimable Lady Ashland were stuffed up together in the carriage.

"Likely she does," she answered. "It is my understanding that such… situations are not uncommon among the upper classes."

Devil take it, but she was galling. "You're certainly free in disparaging my class, yet quite defensive of any remarks on your own." He could feel her bristling and almost—*almost*—took enjoyment in riling her.

She was right, though he wouldn't give her the satisfaction of saying so. His father was not the first man of his or any class to take a mistress. It just seemed an occasional fling was a hell of a difference from having an entire second family established.

Mrs. Goodson's house stood picture-perfect in a leafy glade. It was not a large house, or an imposing one, and had nothing of the majesty and history of Ashland Park. But even from the carriage window it was obvious that the home was well-tended and cared for. The gravel drive was clean and freshly raked, the lawn clipped, the hedges trimmed. There were flowers everywhere. Even the rain let up as they approached, and a shaft of weak sunlight broke through the murky skies. Naturally.

They rolled to a stop before the modest home and Ash took a breath. It might have been the Palace for all the emotion roiling in his gut. But inside that turmoil was an equal amount of indignation and something he hadn't yet examined. He steadied himself and exited the carriage.

With a critical eye he examined the exterior of the home, noting the state of repair. There was no fading paint, no broken window panes, no crumbling mortar. It was, in short, in excellent condition.

The door opened before they reached it, and a woman stepped out, gazing at them coolly. "My lord Ashland," she said, her accent surprisingly refined, and that is how Ash met his father's mistress.

* * *

"You have the look of your father," she said, bold as can be, as she poured out the tea in the drawing room to which they'd adjourned. She moved with comfortable grace, showing no outward sign of discomfort or shame in their presence.

The room, while small, was cozy and clean, filled with comfortable furnishings. A large picture window looked out over a pretty garden, hills and green fields stretched out beyond it.

"I am told I favor my mother," Ash said, both because it was somewhat true and to remind this woman of her place. Honora glanced at him, but said nothing.

Mrs. Goodson inclined her head, as though giving the matter some thought. Objectively, if he'd been forced, he could say she was a woman in fine looks, though she appeared to be in her late 30's. She'd a pleasant face, dark blonde hair done up in a sleek chignon, a plush, generous figure and a bosom that positively dominated the entire front of her.

She was, Ash realized with a start of revulsion, just the type of woman he typically preferred. He cast a glance at his wife, her fine-boned, dark-haired presence an antidote to the thought.

"You seem remarkably unsurprised to find us at your door," he said, leaving his teacup untouched. It was hardly a moment for food, although if pressed, he would consider the possibility of availing himself of a cake or two.

"It did seem inevitable that your curiosity would eventually win out over your distaste."

"Actually, I only learned of your existence yesterday, courtesy of the countess." He indicated Honora with his head.

"I was unaware that my husband was ignorant of the situation, Mrs. Goodson," she explained. "I'm certain you can understand the news has come as something of a shock. But perhaps you would be willing to clarify a few details for us?"

She appeared only too happy to do so, and in short order Mrs. Goodson sketched out the details of her life with the late earl: she was a twenty-year-old actress when they'd met; he'd bought her this house fifteen years ago, upon the birth of their first son; he'd visited her three or four times a week up until the day he died.

"Every summer we traveled to the seaside," she said, a hint of wistfulness emerging. "He was a wonderful man."

It was at this point that Ash began to feel a bit ill with the emotions coursing through him. Anger, chiefly. He'd never taken a trip with his father. Even when he'd gone away to school for the first time, it had been in the company of servants. There had been no affection or friendship and he hadn't even thought he'd wanted it until he'd heard this woman talking about it. His father had barely spared any time for him, and even less for Margaret, who was unfortunate enough to have been born a girl.

"James is away at school," Mrs. Goodson was saying, watching him guardedly, "but Jonathan is still at home."

"James. And Jonathan." And Jasper, his own given name, though anyone rarely used it. A perfectly matched set of three brothers. "Christ." He stood and went to the window, wanting to put his fist through it.

"Perhaps I could bring him in?"

Ash didn't answer. He couldn't. After a moment, Honora cleared her throat and replied, "Yes. Of course."

"They don't know about you," she cautioned. "About any of this."

Mrs. Goodson left the room, and shortly Honora approached him, putting a hand tentatively on his arm. "You aren't going to hit anyone, are you?"

He shrugged. "This window, perhaps. It's so bloody clean."

"We should move them to Ashland as punishment."

Ash laughed, he couldn't help it, and some of his tension dissipated. They stood that way for a moment, staring out at the garden.

"I'd like to know where he found the money to keep them," Honora said, disapproval writ clear in her voice.

"I'd like to know how he found the time, or the energy, or the inclination." She actually gave his arm a reassuring little squeeze, an act he found both ridiculous and oddly touching.

"She is a very…attractive type of woman." She coughed a bit and he turned to find her biting her lip. "She is concerned we will cut her off."

Ash was actually shocked. "You mean to say the estate is supporting her still?"

Honora nodded. "Until yesterday I assumed you were sanctioning it."

"I most certainly am not," he bit out. "She can find her own damn—" He stopped as Mrs. Goodson came back into the room, her son in tow.

She guided the boy into the room, her hands on his shoulders, an unmistakable look of pride lighting her eyes. "This is Jonathan."

He was a small fellow, nonchalantly peering up at them from under a mop of golden-brown hair. He'd a smudge of dirt above his jaw, despite an obvious last-minute scrubbing. And though his eyes were his mother's, the shape of his head, the set of his shoulders, the impudent quirk of his lip were all his father's, and Ash could clearly see the old man in the child, and a startling, undeniable resemblance to himself.

Ash broke the moment of silence. "Do you know who I am, boy?" The lad shook his head. "I am the Earl of Ashland and I am your brother."

Mrs. Goodson actually gasped, and young Jonathan gave him a suspicious look. "My brother is at school."

"Yes, he is, but I am your other brother. Our father saw fit to keep two families, yours and mine."

"How dare you!" His mother exclaimed, grasping her son by the arm, ready to pluck him from the room. Honora watched him with a growing frown.

"I dare, Mrs. Goodson. I'd say he's the right to the truth, now and not when he's full grown. He'll know he's a bastard, and whose." Mrs. Goodson turned purple.

"Ashland!" His wife twitched, and he thought she was about a second away from attempting to physically restrain him.

Young Jonathan, however, watched him steadily. "Tommy Morris said to James he was a bastard." Mrs. Goodson took a shaky breath and began to cry.

"There!" Ash exclaimed, throwing up his hands. "The neighbors already know, and now so do you, and they can't wield any power over you." Jonathan nodded sagely. "And the next time anyone calls you a bastard, you tell them you are the son and brother of an earl. And...if you need to, you come and find me when you're grown."

With that, Ashland turned and made for the door. Enough was enough for one day. He could hear his wife making hasty goodbyes, and then she was rushing out the door behind him. They hurried through the downpour, and into the waiting carriage.

CHAPTER SIX

ᏛᎦ

T hey rode without speaking for a long time. The carriage trudged along the muddy roads as Honora gazed out of the window at the rain, head lolling in time with the rocking of the vehicle. Ashland eventually broke the silence.

"He had to know the truth. I gave him sound advice," he said, almost defensively. He was stretched out across from her, arms folded across his chest, staring at nothing.

Honora mulled over this pronouncement. "I agree—" he shot her a mocking look "—with the first part." His expression turned surly. "But, in hindsight, one might consider the news better delivered from the child's mother, at a time of her choosing, and not from a strange man suddenly appearing in one's drawing room. An *earl*, no less."

Ashland's lips twitched, the natural up-turn of his mouth lifting into a complete smile, and then, suddenly and quite unexpectedly, he was laughing. Seeing her puzzlement, he laughed even harder, until he was gasping for breath.

"Oh, God, you're right!" he wheezed. "What the devil was I thinking?"

A swell of answering laughter started in her chest and burst forth, until she too was practically snorting in mirth. They laughed that way until her side hurt. She sighed, wiping her eye.

"That is a failure on your part," he said. She looked at him, curious. "To let me go on with such pomposity. Where was your command, madam?"

"I daresay lost in the shock of the moment." A lingering giggle escaped her.

They stopped at an inn for lunch, tarrying over the meal in hopes that the rain would let up. It was a surprisingly good meal, and Honora ate her fill, even accepting a glass of wine. "Much needed, I should think, after the day's events," she answered in response to Ashland's raised brow.

After a while she again broached the subject of Mrs. Goodson.

"Will you tell your mother and sister about her?"

He chewed for a while before answering. "No," he said finally, tossing the corner of his bread onto the plate. "It would devastate them."

Here she knew to tread carefully. "Mightn't it be more devastating to keep it from them?" she sipped at her wine. "To let the secret fester."

He shook his head and spoke with finality. "I cannot tell them."

Honora accepted his answer and then, since she was already discussing such sensitive matters, mentioned Mrs. Goodson's financial support.

Ashland laughed harshly. "My own damn estate is crumbling around my ears, and she wants money." He stared moodily at his wine.

"Yes, well, she will need to feed the children." He shot her a glance indicating his lack of appreciation for her statement. "They are not to be blamed for their parentage. Cutting off their mother will devastate them as well, and won't provide you with any revenge against your father."

He continued staring down at his fingers, twisting the wine glass round and round on the table. After a moment he looked up, staring at her. "Do you really believe I would destroy the lives of innocent children, my own brothers, no less, all for the sake of revenge?" he asked roughly.

Honora opened her mouth. That was precisely what she thought, but he was watching her so oddly, that she reconsidered admitting it. "I don't know, do I?" she said instead. "I don't know what kind of man you are. We have only been married for a matter of weeks, and we remain strangers to one another. I do not know what you are capable of."

"Too true, too true," he nodded, and for some reason she'd the queerest sensation that he was disappointed. "Alas, I am only a careless ne'er-do-well, and no villain. I've no talent for starving mothers and their children. On that count, you may rest assured."

He signaled to the innkeeper and they were off shortly after, the tentative ease between them acutely soured.

* * *

After another hour of being jostled inside the muggy carriage with her sullen spouse, Honora wanted nothing more than to retire to the relative sanctuary of her rooms. Her head ached after the prolonged journey brought on by the muddy roads, and she planned to immediately go to her bedchamber and put on her dressing gown.

Instead, as they approached the house, Ash craned his head to peer out the window, and said, "What in bloody hell is happening now?"

It turned out that the vast rainfall had been the death knell for the rotting roof of the east wing. Even from the carriage they could see that an entire section of the roof had simply caved in under the latest round of moisture. The wing was uninhabited, but served as storage to family mementos and old paperwork, items having been spared the selling-block by virtue of lacking any resale value.

It was still a disaster. The rain would ruin the walls, weaken the floors, and hamper the restoration process that was finally beginning to make headway. Mr. Perkins had fortunately responded quickly, sending as many hands as he could to the scene, but there was little to be done. "We have been removing as much as we could from the rooms, my lord," he told Ash, jogging to meet them as they exited the carriage, "until the floors began groaning, and I thought it best to evacuate." Mr. Perkins cast a forlorn, wounded glance at the house, taking this mishap as a personal affront.

With no way to cover the gaping hole in the roof, Honora and Ashland stood on the lawn, along with Mr. Perkins and the entire staff, helplessly watching the rain pour into the east wing. To Honora, it felt like rubbing salt into the wound. It may have been far from well-maintained, but there was something deeply cutting about seeing the house collapsing before their eyes. All of the work and progress so far seemed for naught, and she fought a tremendous urge to stamp her foot into the muddy ground.

She looked at Ashland. He stood perfectly still, gaze unflinching from the house, his expression grimmer than she'd ever seen it. He hadn't said a word after Perkin's report. There was obviously nothing to be done. His utter stillness spoke volumes, and she struggled for words of comfort, but none came to mind.

It began to grow dark, and the staff slowly moved indoors, to the stable, to dry parts of the house. The rain continued unabated and Honora stood her ground at Ashland's side, until only the two of them remained on the soggy lawn. She wanted desperately to go indoors as well, but could not leave him until the spell that seemed to have taken hold of him broke. Still he stared at the house, which grew harder and harder to see, the lowering dark concealing some of the damage. Honora thought he might stand that way until the rain stopped. By this point she was absolutely drenched; water rolled in a steady rivulet down the back of her gown, flowing in a chilly stream directly against her spine.

She turned to him, laying a heavy hand against his arm. "We will catch our death in this rain." She could barely see his features anymore, but felt the tense rigidity under her fingertips. "Let us go indoors."

He was quiet for a long moment and then took a breath so deep and shuddering that she feared his lungs had already succumbed to inflammation. "It might be easier if it just burned down," he said. "What a hell of a day."

When at long last they entered the house, the servants were upon them, ushering Honora and Ashland to their respective chambers, where merry fires and dry towels awaited them. Honora let Poppy remove her clothing, no easy task with the sodden garments. Honora stared numbly into the flames as Poppy struggled, abruptly drained by the warmth and blessed respite from the downpour outside.

A hell of a day, indeed. She'd been filled with tension since morning, and filled with dread since he'd announced his plans to visit Mrs. Goodson. And then the sight of Ashland falling on itself... She let out a long breath, and stared into the fire, thoughts whirling.

Nothing had gone as she'd imagined. Honora had been so puzzled by Ash's behavior at Mrs. Goodson's house. Didn't all aristocrats keep mistresses? Was not that the way of their urbane world? Yet the existence of Mrs. Goodson and the children had hurt him, she was sure of it, and Honora could not reconcile this with the man who thus far had exhibited only a careless inattention to all things familial.

Would Ashland one day have a mistress of his own, she wondered? She supposed he must, that he was bred to a certain outlook and expectations. A rather unpleasant feeling flared in her chest at the thought. Her views were provincial, she was sure, and indicative of her inferior background. She was not fanciful enough (or fool enough, Granny would certainly say) to believe in some hare-brained notion of marrying for love, but neither was she sophisticated enough to blithely tolerate her husband cavorting with another woman. She doubted she ever would be.

Above all else, Honora wanted children. The only child of an only child, she'd immediately become the sole hope for the future of the Botham Family interests when her parents died. All of Granny's considerable aspirations had been pinned on Honora's bony shoulders, and from the time she'd become orphaned at the tender age of ten, Honora's life had been an exercise in preparation to one day assume control of the family's weighty empire.

It wasn't that Granny didn't love her. She did, fiercely, but there hadn't been much place for tenderness or affection with Granny. By passing on her business knowledge and training Honora to her rigid and elevated standards, she'd done her level best for her granddaughter. Granny knew there was no room for a delicate gentlewoman in a man's world; the best thing she could do for her was to raise her with the most realistic of expectations.

It had worked. Honora was exceptionally qualified to take control of all aspects of Botham Enterprises upon Granny's passing four years ago. The businesses had thrived, and Honora felt the warm sense of pride and satisfaction that she was the one nurturing it all. Granny's goals were achieved: She'd successfully taken control of the business and married a title.

But motherhood, motherhood was Honora's goal. Children, the deepest wish of her heart. She would love them freely and not teach them about the business until they were older. They would have siblings and affection and ridiculous freedom to run through the countryside like tiny madmen. She would allow them all the things that were denied her.

But children required a father, and thus far the begetting of an heir did not seem high on Lord Ashland's list of priorities. Honora frowned, glancing out the window at the inky lawns, stifling the feeling that she was running out of time.

Their intimate encounters thus far were infrequent and dismally unfulfilling. She certainly felt the requisite way; merely being in his presence could spark that melting heat in her belly that spread to the core of her, but in the end, left her dissatisfied and uncertain. Honora did not deal in uncertainty and here was a problem, but she did not understand its cause.

How was she to have children when they could not seem to deal with each other at all? And what would become of her if he did take a mistress, and spent his time in her bed? What recourse would she possibly have? Nothing, save her money and her new-found title, neither of which would provide much comfort or consolation.

Exhausted and thoroughly dispirited, she fell into bed, visions of Mrs. Goodson standing in the collapsing house plaguing her dreams.

* * *

Were it not for the look on Margaret's face—that hopeful, expectant, happy gleam she had taken on since his marriage to the heiress—Ashland would have certainly packed up and ridden back to London at first light. Hell, he might even go now, in the middle of this wet and wretched night, throwing all sense and caution to the wind. He hated Ashland Park. Quite thoroughly and sincerely despised it. It was a moldering, decrepit millstone around his neck, symbolic of the failure of generations of Ashland men. It was, in quite the most literal way, falling down about their ears.

But Margaret, nineteen and already a year behind her season, Margaret needed him, and he very much doubted his wife would continue to fund any season or the requisite accoutrements thereof if he vanished.

Instead, a sense of being put-upon, bolstered by no small amount of brandy, led him to the conclusion that the east wing required immediate inspection. With crystal decanter in hand, he made his way through dark hallways and a good deal of house until he found himself standing in a puddle at the edge of the corridor leading into the now-ruined wing. He couldn't see much from this vantage point, but could hear the rain falling. It smelled of dank water here, and cold air billowed freely throughout the corridor, twisting around his ankles like an icy hand. He took a deep swig of the brandy and tap-tap-tapped his toe against the drenched rug.

"This is an HEIRLOOM!" he shouted into the dark, empty corridor, his words disappearing into the damp. "It's... Aubusson," he slurred, lifting the brandy decanter to his mouth. A pleasant wave of heat moved down his throat as he swallowed.

He could not recall the last time he'd been in the east wing. Very likely it was as a child, for the east wing had made a perfect playground. "And now it's gone," he said. Or not quite. If it were gone, say destroyed in a fire or collapsed into a heap, then they could clean up the debris and continue with the restoration of the remainder of the house. But here it still stood, neither intact nor demolished, an invalid in desperate need of attention.

In need. He laughed. It should be the Ashland family motto.

A fresh draft wafted around his ankles. The corridor yawned before him like a dark maw, more than ready to swallow him up. And it would. The corridor, the house, the earldom and all that was Ashland would consume him whole and spit out a pile of splintery bones. He took an unsteady step toward the black mouth, ready to embrace the darkness before it came for him.

"Easy!" A hand shot out from behind him and gripped his wrist, stopping him in his tracks. He tottered and turned around, both surprised and not, to find his wife staring at him in concern, her fine black brows drawn tightly together. "Ah, my countess!" There was enough moonlight spilling through the tall windows to reveal she was in her nightclothes, a voluminous white nightgown that engulfed her from neck to toes. "As alluring as ever."

She dropped his wrist and took a step back. "On second thought, do proceed." She indicated the destroyed hallway before him, and turned to leave.

"Wait," he sighed, and then repeated himself when she made no move to do so. "Wait!" he yelled, and she halted and turned, inclining her head at him in an exaggerated fashion. "I..."

Just at that moment, something came down with a huge crash, shaking the walls and floor. Honora flinched, bringing her arms over her ears, and Ashland hit the ground. Bits of plaster rained down on them, and a cloud of dust and debris shot out of the corridor, where suddenly the sound of rain was much louder.

"Move!" Ash shouted at her, and then leapt for her when she did not stir. He sprang up, grabbing her around the waist and sprinting away from the crash. He didn't run far. It only needed a few steps to get away from the entrance to the east wing and its spewing miasma. Whatever happened had been further down the corridor. Already the dust was dissipating, though the stench of rot and decay had increased tenfold.

He turned to look at his wife, whom he'd wedged between himself and the wall. She faced away from him, her arms still tight over her ears, her shoulders hunched and tense. She was probably terrified.

"Are you alright?" he asked.

She coughed, then lowered her arms and turned around, looking at him coolly. She looked no more ruffled than she ever did, only as serene and unconcerned as though she were taking a morning stroll.

"Perfectly," she answered, cocking her head as she looked up at him. With his arms cage-like about her and their bodies pressed close together, she had nowhere to lower her hands other than onto his chest. This she did gingerly, reluctant to really touch him.

He laughed shortly. "Does nothing ever disturb your composure?" It was a trait both admirable and annoying.

She ignored his question. "What do you think happened?"

He glanced over his shoulder at the black hole behind them. "More of the roof fell in. And I seem to have lost my brandy. Damn." The decanter lay on the floor, its contents sadly disgorged all over the rug. He turned back to her, to find her watching him with a new expression, no less discomposed than her usual façade, but with an edge of something that hadn't been there a moment before. Her glance fell to his mouth, and he became suddenly, intensely aware of the way their bodies pressed together.

The entire front of her body was tight against his, and nothing between them save the layers of her nightgown, thin linen that did little to cushion the shape of her beneath. He could feel her distinctly against his flesh, unexpected contours and softness.

"I suppose this isn't quite the life you'd imagined, as a countess. Collapsing houses and all that." As he spoke, he slowly pushed one arm tighter against her, waiting for a reproach. When none came, he pressed himself closer against her, moving his hips in the slightest way.

She inhaled and her hands clenched on his chest.

"You must have wished for the life of luxury that should befit your new status." He swiveled his hips again and his cock came fully to life, growing hard in a second. She continued to watch his mouth, her gaze finally beginning to soften, her own lips parting in a damp pink bow.

"Alas," he traced a hand along her side, gliding from waist to breast, slowly, and back again. He felt as though he were weaving a spell upon her, and he liked it. For once she seemed incapable of the wise or judicious or cutting retorts that seemed to endlessly flow from her mouth.

He drew his hand upward, cupping her. The small breast fit entirely in his palm, the nipple hard against his hand. He could see the point of the other one through her nightgown and it was, he admitted to himself with some wonder, an enticing sight.

Hell, any breast, even one so small, was bound to be appealing.

She seemed to like it, for she arched against him and bit her lip. She watched him through half-closed eyes, breathing in hot little bursts that caressed his cheek. Her expression altered, aloofness replaced by something completely different, unguarded softness and heat. Ash's cock throbbed in response and he ground himself against the place between her legs, which had spread invitingly open.

This motion elicited an altogether gratifying response, a sound the cross between a squeak and a moan, and Honora's arm moved around his shoulders as she angled herself for better support.

It was all Ash needed. He lowered his hand from her breast to the hem of her nightgown, raising it up well past her hips. With his free hand he quickly undid his buttons until his cock sprang out, ready and greedy. He stroked himself a few times, growing even harder, and then positioned himself at her entrance, holding the nightgown bunched around her waist. With a groan he pushed into her warmth in one long, even thrust.

"What..." She made a sound, but he was thrusting, insensate to anything but the longing for release that had taken over him. He could feel it building, his balls tightening as he stroked and stroked into her heat, harder and harder until it was upon him and he was coming, groaning into her neck.

He stood that way for a moment, pressing her against the wall as the pleasure rode over him in waves, ebbing and flowing in decreasing bursts.

Once he'd caught his breath he raised his head and looked down at her.

It had been an astonishingly stimulating encounter. Her gown was still bunched up between them, and her hair had become a disheveled cloud. Her hands lay flat against his chest. He looked at the place where they were joined, her legs pale and soft against his flesh. Finally he looked up at her face.

The soft, melting look was gone. Her expression was back to its usual cool remoteness, only now it was tinged with something that could easily be labeled disappointment, if he hadn't known better.

* * *

The next few days were harried and exhausting, rushing from one disaster to the next. The damage to the estate was slow to be assessed; it was too dangerous for anyone to venture too deeply into the sodden east wing, lest they meet their doom under a collapsing beam or rotten floor. They explored in short bursts, edging along the destruction with the respect due a sleeping tiger: with small steps and very quietly.

Ash worked with the rest of them. It was, in fact, a job for all hands and virtually every able-bodied man on the estate was pulled in to assist with the task. Footmen and farmers, workmen and stable boys, errand boys and village lads stood elbow to elbow with the earl himself in an attempt to salvage anything possible from the debris.

And Ash was astonished to find how much the long-neglected east wing actually contained. Someone, probably his grandmother, in an attempt to save something from her wastrel husband, had taken advantage of the abandoned place and hidden all manner of treasure: paintings, silver, furniture, rugs and clothing were tucked away here and there. At points the rescue began to feel like a dismal archaeological excavation. A few of the treasures survived, but most were destroyed, or had probably been in an advanced state of decay even before the roof collapse.

Irritatingly, as he worked, Ash found his thoughts wandering with a tiresome regularity to his wife and the expression on her face that night in the moonlit hallway. It was nothing, he told himself, a trick of the shadows, and then he'd recall the sour twist to her lip, and wonder what could have caused it. He recalled the surprising heat of their encounter, and the sense of satisfaction that her disagreeable look had washed away.

It was nothing, it was everything.

His annoyance with himself grew. What did he care for her looks or sour disposition? He tried to convince himself it did not matter, but the constant repetition of his thoughts told him otherwise. He felt as though he'd quite missed something, and he'd no idea what.

And then the back-breaking job would take over and wipe all the thoughts from his mind, for a while, until they returned again.

Fortunately, he was able to avoid her, as she was in another part of the house, helping sort and deal with anything they were able to rescue. It was here that he found her four days after the disaster, peering with intense scrutiny at one of the paintings they'd unearthed, a small, prettily-framed portrait of some dead ancestor.

Standing overly close and peering intensely at her was the architect, the Mr. Somebody or other she'd hired to oversee the initial restoration that had now been put on hold by the destruction of the east wing. The man was watching her with a look Ash knew all too well, and stood mere inches away from her ear, inhaling the scent of her hair.

Ash stopped in his tracks, taking in the scene before him. Something odd and unpleasant twisted deep in his gut, and he felt a strong need to box the man's nose.

"Interesting find?" he asked instead from his post at the door.

The architect jumped and looked ready to swallow his tongue when he saw Ash. He backed hastily away, clearly trying to find a way to distance himself from the countess without appearing to do so. His wife kept her eye glued to the portrait.

"M-my lord!"

Ash glared at the man. He did not like him standing so close to Honora. And he particularly did not like this sensation of possessiveness that had swept over him upon him the sight. It stirred up a slew of feelings he'd rather never scrutinize.

"Simpson," Ash said curtly, never moving his gaze from the architect as he stepped toward him.

"S-simmons, my lord," he corrected, backing into the edge of a table, sending the lamp atop it teetering.

Ash glared harder.

"This is really quite extraordinary," his wife exclaimed.

Simmons turned his eyes upon her again, then looked at the painting, then back at Ash. He paled.

"Mr. Simmons, I trust your services could be of better use elsewhere," Ash said, nearly baring his teeth at the man. He did not want this anemic architect looking at his wife. Furthermore, he really was quite overcome with the urge to smash his fist into the man's face and wanted him gone from the room before he did so.

Simmons bowed hastily and nearly fell over his own feet fleeing the room, but the urge to violence still coursed through Ash's veins. He'd never felt anything like this in his life and he certainly did not appreciate feeling it now.

"Extraordinary," Honora repeated, finally managing to turn some of his attention away from the hot anger that coursed through him. He looked at her, wondering how much of her indifference to Simmons's slavering proximity was an act.

"What the devil is happening here?" he shouted.

This got her attention. She turned her head, startled. "Are you shouting at me?"

He wanted to shout some more, but wasn't exactly sure what it was he wanted to say. "It appears I am," he answered. He wanted to scold her about that blasted architect yet at the same time did not want her to know the jealous turn his thoughts had taken. It all made him angrier.

She tilted her head at him, bemused, obviously waiting for an explanation. After a moment she sighed and frowned, perplexed. "This ordeal has plainly taken its toll on you."

"Ordeal? I'm afraid with the assortment of ordeals to which I've recently been party that you will need to clarify. Do you refer to my compulsory nuptials? The collapse of my ancestral home? Or perhaps the discovery of my father's secret second family? The mistress and illegitimate sons? Do be specific."

Honora bit her lip. That glint, the one he'd glimpsed when they'd laughed in the carriage, that glint was there, and a sparkle in her eye, and he thought that she would laugh again, and he did not want her laughter. He was in no mood to be mollified.

He turned his attention to the painting she'd been examining, the *pièce de résistance* which had caused the architect to sniff her hair. "What's this?"

"Ah," she breathed, taking in the picture anew. It really was a pretty thing: a woman of middle years, surrounded by four children of various ages and two dogs. The overall affect was somewhat unusual, though if asked he would not be able to say why. There was something different to the technique than the standard portraiture which graced this and most other houses, yet the difference only added to the realism of the piece. The woman's eyes pierced right through him and he fought the urge to look away, much as one would from a staring person.

"It is undoubtedly one of your ancestors, a mother and her children. What strikes me is the style, most singular. It is breathtaking." She traced a hand over the painting, not quite touching it. "Her gaze is so powerful. She looks out at the viewer, yet the love for her children is palpable."

Ash glanced down at the painting. She was right. The woman looked straight at him while the children frolicked around her, but the love she bore for her children was somehow conveyed, and the chief emotion of the picture. He looked back at Honora, staring fixedly at the mother and children. All he could think of was Mrs. Goodson and her boys, his father's other sons, with whom he had holidayed on the seashore.

"To think it was nearly destroyed," Honora sighed.

Ashland sighed, rubbing a hand over his face. He was bone-tired and did not care about paintings or relics or really anything at all at the moment. He didn't know why he'd come in here, only that he wanted to be elsewhere.

The sense of detachment he'd been keeping at bay reared up and seized him; he could no longer fight it off. Nor did he desire to. In that instant it washed away the dread and panic that had been throttling him for so long. Like shears snipping a thread, he felt it all slipping away.

"Take it," he muttered. "Do with it what you will."

CHAPTER SEVEN

Honora descended from the carriage and stepped onto the pavement before her London house. She looked up at its cherished façade: the pristine stairs; the polished black door; the numerous windows sparkling in the late afternoon sun. The homes on her street were too new to be considered the height of fashion. It was most often described as too garish, too vulgar, too full of newly rich men with grasping wives and daughters. Too full of people like Honora herself. It was precisely what the old establishment, the good *ton* aristocracy of her new family, most despised: moneyed upstarts with no sense of place. Honora adored it.

The street was deserted at the moment, and therefore unusually quiet. Her neighbors' doors were shut, the green empty. She breathed in the familiar complex scents of London in early spring and knew she was home. Though she longed to get inside, she lingered a moment on the peaceful walk, quietly bracing herself for the encounter to come.

In the twenty-five days since she'd last seen Ashland, since he had made his craven, secretive departure from Ashland Park, she had imagined many ways in which she might cause him bodily harm. She attempted to quell that urge, now that their reunion was upon her. It was no easy task, for the fantasies of slapping him had provided a great deal of enjoyment to her in the last month, toiling away in the country.

Alas, the door was opening, the butler, Neville, throwing it wide in welcome, and she had to gather her wits. The footmen poured forth in the frenzied process of unloading the trunks and getting everything into the house.

"Welcome home, my lady!" Neville said as she moved past him into the foyer, and though his taciturn expression betrayed not a hint of emotion, she knew he was glad to see her.

"It is good to be home, Neville! I feel I've been gone an age." Oh, she had dearly missed her house. With the familiarity of long-standing habit, she removed her bonnet and tossed it on the side table.

"I trust you've kept everything running smoothly, Neville," Honora said, tossing her gloves onto the table as well, noticing a stack of calling cards on the silver tray that stood there. "Ruled with an iron fist and all that."

"Of course, my lady," he responded dryly, helping her off with her coat as two footmen squeezed past to the stairwell with her largest trunk. "Floggings abounded. You should know—"

"Is his lordship at home?" Honora asked. She remained outwardly composed, though her heart seemed to beat in her throat, squeezed there by the anger that coursed through her at the thought of him blithely entertaining his friends while she labored at Ashland.

"His lordship? I cannot say. Easy there!" he called out to the footmen as the trunk thumped the wall. "However, my lady—"

"Did he not say when he'd return?" Honora poked a finger in the calling cards, sending them toppling.

"I cannot say, he has not been here."

"What do you mean?" Honora turned to the butler, suddenly feeling like they were having two separate conversations. Over his shoulder, she could see Poppy through the open door, dressing down one of the footman for his rough handling of the hatboxes while the coachman fussed with handing over the horses to the groom.

"He is not in residence, if that is what you are inquiring, but there is a matter—"

Honora turned to stare at the butler, a sensation of dread taking root in her stomach. "Not in residence? What do you mean? He left Ashland

Park nearly a month ago." She'd assumed he'd been here in the meantime, and now it seemed her butler was telling her otherwise. She opened her mouth to question Neville more, but just at that moment the drawing room doors opened, revealing the dowager countess and a room full of women behind her. Honora's questions froze in her throat.

"Honora. My dear. You have returned." Lady Celeste's convivial tone belied the look of disappointment in her eye, blocked from her guests fanned out behind her like a 'V' of curious geese. "You simply must join us."

"Lady Celeste is entertaining guests in the drawing room," Neville finished under his breath, and took a solid step away from her. She was on her own.

Honora stared at the dowager, somehow having forgotten that both she and Margaret were living here. Quite frankly, with everything that had happened over the last few weeks, she'd given little thought to the two women, and when she did, she vaguely pictured them going about their own business in their own rooms, not here, entertaining guests in her drawing room, and certainly not confronting her minutes after she walked in the door after a wearying journey.

Furthermore, her head was spinning with the news that Ashland was not in residence. If he wasn't here, then were in the devil was he?

Lady Celeste was silently willing her to go away. But her coterie, the gaggle of women behind her, watched Honora with a familiar look of silent judgement: if she refused to join them, they would condemn her as inhospitable, possibly even haughty. She'd no choice but to enter the drawing room, so with a dip of her head and against the honest wishes of herself and the dowager, she did just so.

They watched her as she entered, each one taking her measure from head to toe with varying degrees of subtlety. Still in her wrinkled traveling costume, she knew she made a dusty and disheveled picture. She could feel tendrils of her hair slipping out at the nape of her neck and lifted her chin, fighting the urge to fix it.

The women were spread out around her drawing room, with tea and cakes. Lady Celeste made the introductions; many of the names were familiar, though she'd never before been introduced to any of them. Indeed, before this day, they would have been unlikely to address her in public, so rigid were their notions of superiority.

All the while, Honora's brain churned, wondering where Ashland was.

She'd awoken one morning to the astonishing news that he had taken a horse and left Ashland Park. That had been just over three weeks ago. It had taken Honora that long to stabilize the numerous ventures at Ashland enough to be free to leave the old heap and return to town. Weeks of tying up loose ends and making sure that all the various projects were at a functioning level had done little for her disposition. She'd been planning on giving the earl an earful about his negligence, and now she'd nowhere to dispel her ire.

The room was stifling. A coal fire burned unnecessarily in the grate, the resultant fug of smoke permeating the space like a bleak cloud. Lady Celeste, she supposed, wanted to assure her friends that she could afford random fires, though more than one of them was looking rather flushed from the heat.

Amazing, really, how one could keep up a trivial exchange while the mind was otherwise engaged. Honora responded with the proper trivialities: Oh, yes; Very well, indeed; I would be delighted to, all while her mind churned over the issue with Ashland, and planned. Did he think to bury her in the country while he gallivanted in town? Well, she was not some simpering, helpless wife, fresh from her father's house, groomed to obey like a loyal hound. She was a woman grown, and one not overly tolerant of nonsense.

"My dear?" Honora's attention shifted to Lady Celeste, who must have been attempting to capture her attention, for she watched her oddly. "You must be exhausted from your travels. I daresay no one would think it odd if you wished to retire." The other women nodded, and Honora realized she had been more lost in thought than she'd realized.

She made a pretty apology, with promises to call, and finally, blessedly, ascended to the privacy of her rooms.

* * *

It did not take long to realize several things: Lady Celeste and Margaret, while relatively small in physical stature, lived in a large fashion. Honora was astounded that two women could accumulate so many things and make so much noise. The house positively vibrated with their presence, in a curious contrast to the glum silence that had pervaded Ashland Park. They were either coming or going or planning on doing so, and even when they rested it was with a considerable amount of fanfare. Fans needed to be fetched, cushions moved, curtains drawn—silence had become a thing of the past.

Their social calendar was extensive. There were calls and balls, parties and rides, breakfasts, shopping trips and teas. Endless rounds of shopping. Honora observed them much as a bemused spectator watching a play, wondering how many clever bonnets one woman could need.

Flowers and invitations were delivered with frequency, making the foyer one of the busiest rooms in the house.

Another item of discovery, and one much to Honora's astonishment, was Lady Celeste's disapproval over Ashland's absence. Honora would have assumed that the issue was not one the woman would care to concern herself with, but she had taken immediate umbrage at Ashland's behavior.

The minute she'd learned of her son's defection, her mouth had tightened into a thin line and a half-frown marked her brow.

"Do you mean to say, Honora," she had asked at breakfast that first morning, after she had inquired as to Ashland's whereabouts, "that my son has separated from you?" The room was redolent with the scent of toast, bacon and coffee. Bright morning light streamed through the tall windows.

"He returned to London without me. You may call it what you will." Honora spread jam on a piece of toast. Though it galled her to admit as much to her mother-in-law, she could hardly pretend to know his whereabouts.

Lady Celeste's grasp on her fork tightened. "What reason did he give you?"

"None." Honora shrugged. "He simply...left."

The dowager took a deep, shaky breath. "This is most unacceptable."

Honora paused with the toast halfway to her mouth. It was the most emotion she'd ever seen the dowager demonstrate.

"That a man of his station should so publicly cast aside his new bride! It is degrading to the Ashland name."

Naturally, Honora thought. The Ashland name would take precedence over the slight to the aforementioned new bride.

"This is strawberry jam," Honora said, having at last bitten into the toast.

"Indeed."

"But I prefer raspberry."

Lady Celeste gave her an impatient look.

Disappointed, Honora put down the toast. She always had raspberry jam with her toast. She looked around, but the footman was not to be found. It appeared that the Dowager's changes had infiltrated the kitchens as well, a most displeasing notion. "Am I to conclude, then" Honora sighed, "that you do not know where Ashland is keeping himself?"

Lady Celeste shook her head and took a half-bite of egg. "I can only assume he has returned to his bachelor lodgings." She paused, for all the world as though searching for a tactful way to say something. "It would not do for it to be known he is living apart from you."

Honora agreed. It would not do. She would not be gossip fodder.

"It might be common knowledge that yours was a marriage of convenience, but one must still put up a good front. It could hamper Margaret's possibilities, and she is so enjoying her season thus far."

Honora bit back a response. Obtuseness appeared a family trait. There was no mention of the amount of work he'd left her with at Ashland, the myriad decisions and directions, for the repairs underway and to the newly collapsed wing, for the tenants, for the staff. They went blithely about their pleasure without a thought to anything that needed to be done. It was no wonder the estate was in such dire straits.

* * *

Prudently deeming it best to remove herself from the house for a while, she decided to pay a long overdue visit to her oldest friend.

"Charlotte Martin!"

"Honora Botham!"

They greeted each other as they'd been doing since their finishing school days, when they'd joked over their shared hierarchical insignificance by loudly and importantly announcing one another's full names. Laughing at their old shared joke, they embraced and looked one another over, reassuring themselves of their mutual well-being.

"That is Lady Sloane, now," Charlotte teased, pulling her into the drawing room. Honora glanced about, taking in the comfortable furnishings and tasteful décor, further satisfying herself that her friend was living in fitting circumstances. There had been no real doubt, but she nevertheless found the sight of the cozy home reassuring.

"And Lady Ashland, if you please," Honora teased back, trying to return Charlotte's smile.

"My word, Honora! A countess! I can hardly credit it." Charlotte tugged her onto the sofa, drawing Honora's hand into her lap to examine her ring. "Is that a family jewel?"

"Indeed," Honora answered. "The ring goes to each new countess at her marriage, along with a mountain of debt and a dilapidated estate."

Charlotte laughed. She herself had been married the year before, to Sir William Sloane, Baronet, an amiable fellow who seemed her perfect match. Sir William held vast lands in the north. Successfully, one might add. Charlotte, the daughter of a gentleman farmer, was considered to have done very well for herself indeed.

"Oh, it has been too long!" Honora said, drinking in the sight of her friend. "I shan't ask you how marriage is treating you, for you are positively beaming."

Charlotte giggled. "I won't deny it." And she could not have; there was about her the proverbial glow that spoke more than words ever could. Everything about her shone, from her skin, to her smile to the mirth in her eyes. Charlotte was happy, and looked the part.

"And little Edward?" Honora asked.

Charlotte's glow, if possible, became even brighter, ringing her in an exultant radiance. "Oh, Honora! I know I should not say it but he is surely the most beautiful baby ever!"

Honora smiled, warmed by her friend's joy. "You aren't going to hide him from me, are you?"

"Indeed not! I will show him off to his auntie as soon as he wakes. But I warn you, you will love him on sight."

Tea was brought in, and the two women settled in for a long chat. What with Charlotte's move to Yorkshire and her confinement, it had been some time since they'd seen one another. Charlotte, with her usual flair for detail, poured and talked, bringing Honora up to date on virtually every facet of her new home, her husband, and infant son. She then turned the topic to Honora.

"I do so wish I could have attended the wedding," she said with a wistful sigh. "Was it magical?"

Honora took a deep drink of her tea, taking a moment to frame her response. Charlotte had been unable to attend the wedding, having only recently given birth. If Honora was honest with herself, as she always endeavored to be, she was glad her dear friend had not been there to see the mockery of her nuptials. Charlotte was in many ways Honora's opposite: petite, blond, full-figured, and she believed in true love and magical weddings and charmed marriages. She always had. She clearly had no regrets in her marriage to Sir William. Honora's situation was considerably different, and she chose her words carefully. Though she'd come hoping to unburden herself to her old friend, she found herself suddenly wanting to guard the less than romantic state of her marriage from happy and romantic Charlotte.

"It will always be a day to remember. I can't say I've ever seen such a ceremony."

Charlotte nearly squealed. "Isn't it wonderful?" she breathed.

Honora bit into a scone and nodded, "Delicious."

"Marriage, you goose! Not tea!" Charlotte scolded. "Oh, you will always tease!"

Honora laughed. "I will. But you are such a good sport about it, Charlotte."

Charlotte glanced at her from beneath her lashes. "And will we be hearing your happy tidings sometime soon?"

Honora sputtered on the scone, and took too long to compose herself. It was certainly a question she should have expected from Charlotte, but the friendly inquiry nevertheless caught her off guard. She feared that if she so much as mentioned a word about her lack of happy tidings, all of her disenchantment would roil forth in an unstoppable flood of pent up emotions.

Sir William came in at that moment, slim and blond, the perfect match to Charlotte's pale coloring. Honora breathed a sigh of relief at his timely interruption and hurried to wipe the crumbs from her fingers before he bowed over her hand in a courtly fashion, and then turned to press a kiss to his wife's cheek.

It was a perfectly respectable embrace in front of an old friend, and yet there was so much more in the gesture: in the way his body leaned towards hers; the way his hand lingered at her waist; the way Charlotte's eyelashes swept downward over pinkened cheeks. Honora read a wealth of affection and desire.

She gazed into her teacup, feigning a fascination with the contents, anything to avoid staring at the doting couple before her, and feeling perhaps more ridiculous than she ever had. She drank her tea, shamefully envious of their ease with one another, their evident delight in each other's presence.

She felt absurdly alone at that moment, excluded from a special society to which she'd likely never belong. All of Honora's family were gone, there was no one left who might reach out and touch her with affection, save Ashland, and he was unlikely to do so. She thought back to their encounter in the corridor at Ashland Park, the marital act devoid of any warmth or actual intimacy. It was the last time anyone had touched her, save Poppy, her maid.

"How is Ashland?" William asked, perching on the arm of Charlotte's chair. "We were at school together," he added, in response to Honora's questioning look.

"Of course," she replied, wondering how to answer such a simple question. She'd no idea if Ashland were doing well or poorly. For all she knew, he could have been making a spectacle of himself the past month, and anything she said could easily be contradicted. She felt a familiar spurt of resentment at her position.

"Very well," she answered with false brightness, for what else could she say. And then she unapologetically changed the topic, asking, "I say, I thought there was a baby to view?"

Both parents became immediately distracted from the subject of Ashland or Honora. The nurse was sent for, and young master Edward promptly produced, a sweet bundle of chubby cheeks and Charlotte's blue eyes, a feathery tuft of yellow hair. Charlotte took him gently from the nurse, gazing at him in rapt wonder. William reached out a hand, cupping the baby's head. They were the very embodiment of familial bliss; the scene only wanted a loyal hound resting at their feet.

"Here's Auntie Honora come to see you," Charlotte cooed, and stood to place him, quite cavalierly Honora thought, into her arms.

Honora stared down, tensing at the unfamiliar weight of such a small creature. He was softer and far more fragile than any child she'd ever held. She dared not move. But oh, he was so beautiful, watching her with placid blue eyes, gnawing on one dimpled fist, seeming to find her the most fascinating thing he'd ever seen.

He was so sweet and tender, and looking into his gaze, something shifted deep inside Honora's core, a deep click of unseen pieces connecting, and she relaxed, feeling for all the world as if she'd been holding tiny babies her entire life. She leaned down and kissed his soft forehead, inhaling his sweet, milky scent. "Eddie," she whispered to him.

As a rule, Honora did not cry. While she did not deem the act of crying a weakness in itself, she knew that anytime a woman produced tears, it served as confirmation to men of their inherent belief in woman's inferiority. Rather than contribute in any way to that particular misapprehension, and because she operated in the world of men, Honora had become expert at biting back tears until crying was simply something she did not do.

But when she left Charlotte, with many warm embraces and promises to return, she hurried into the waiting carriage with an odd stinging sensation at the back of her eyes. She'd come to visit her friend with a hope of assuaging some of her loneliness. Instead, witnessing Charlotte's happiness, witnessing the ordinary affection between a man, wife and child, Honora felt more alone than ever. Charlotte could not commiserate with her, for Charlotte was in a proper marriage. And oh, Honora felt the veriest fool for even making comparisons.

She shifted in her seat and caught a pleasant aroma, Eddie's sweet milky scent from where she'd held him in her arms. The smell brought such a pang of longing to her heart. Her eyes stung anew, and this time, she could not stop the hot tears from overflowing. She leaned her head back against the velvet squabs, and let them come.

CHAPTER EIGHT

There came, at an ungodly hour, a vehement, deranged pounding at his door. Further, a small streak of sunlight had slipped its way through the drawn curtains, hitting his eyes in a devilishly brutal glare.

Pound, pound, pound. The knocking at the door persisted, the shaft of light cut like a blade.

He could turn his head to avoid the light, but the monster at the door seemed unlikely to go away. Just to be sure, he waited another minute, until the fist, or anvil more likely, came down again.

"Aaarrgh!" He made a sound of incoherent pain and fury, and rose from the bed. "That," he yelled, pulling the door open, "is unnecessary!" And then he stopped, speechless, for who should be standing outside his door other than Old Danvers, his landlord, and Honora, Countess of Ashland, his wife.

Old Danvers had at least the grace to look regretful at this breach in confidence—female relatives were not routinely allowed into the lodgings, and privacy was routinely respected. But Honora watched him with a little smirk of spite.

She looked him over, head to toe, taking in his rumpled appearance: last night's trousers, the top button undone, and nothing else. He might be barefoot, shirtless and barely sober, but he nevertheless felt a glimmer of satisfaction when she blushed at the sight of him.

She pushed her way into the room, followed by Danvers, carrying a sizeable packet which he set on the floor before rapidly making his way out again. Ash bowed sarcastically, slamming the door in the landlord's face. Him, he'd deal with later.

It was a reputable lodging, unadorned but fairly clean rooms, but as she passed through he saw the surroundings through her eyes and felt a surge of defensiveness: the tatty furnishings, rumpled clothing littering the floor, the trail of empty bottles.

"So you are back?" he asked.

"Did you think I'd stay at Ashland forever?" She glanced around. "No, I suppose not," she added, more to herself.

It felt as though he had not seen her for a very long time, yet she was at once familiar and strange. He recognized the beginnings of the odd reaction only she seemed to generate in him, a combination of emotions that he chose not to examine.

"Well, I am back, as you so aptly noticed. I was curious as to whether you were yet among the living. And here you are." She gingerly moved a stack of newspapers from the chair and took a seat.

Her gown was more fashionable than anything she'd worn at Ashland, more flounced and detailed, with ribbons and furls, a gown particularly suited to the sophistication of city life. Her hair, likewise, was also more elaborately coiffed, swept back in a complexity of twists and turns that he never seen before. She looked rather well, he realized, trim and elegant. But her eyes, and the impassive look that emitted from them, were the same, and the brief tender feeling within him abruptly faded.

His rooms were small, sparsely furnished with the one chair upon which she was seated, and the bed, where he lowered himself, more out of an inclination to discompose her than anything else. He lay back on the rumpled bedclothes and folded his arms behind his head, crossing his bare feet, vowing to let her speak first. Her gaze slid over his bare chest and away.

"Your mother and sister are well, if by chance you were concerned over their circumstances." A hit. A palpable hit. While he might feel varying shades of obligation to the wife he barely knew, he did feel a deep-seated responsibility to his mother and sister, and his inattention towards them had been the one thorn in his side during the past month.

"I am relieved to know they are tolerating the newness of your house." He knew his mother, and living in one of the crass new-moneyed houses that were popping up all over London must be excruciating for her. A gentlewoman born, she knew the dignity inherent to the older homes and estates of the aristocracy.

"Reasonably well, I should say." She raised a brow at him, unruffled, unaffected, unconcerned. Remarkable. "And you? Have you been keeping well? I notice that the injuries to your nose have healed. One would never guess it was so recently broken. You should consider, perhaps, replacing the charwoman." She glanced again at the untidy room and Ashland almost laughed.

"Ah, the bachelor's life." He stretched, raising his arms high over his head, and was satisfied when she looked away. She might not react to his barbs but she undoubtedly did to his physical presence. She focused her gaze on his feet.

"Far be it from me to remind you of your marital status, but I will speak of your filial obligations."

"I hardly need you to remind me of that!"

"Don't you? Have you even once considered what kind of supervision Margaret has had during her season thus far? Her social calendar is very, very full, and I daresay your mother cannot oversee her at every moment. And in the absence of a male relation, namely you, I fear she is more exposed than she should be."

Her stared at her, aghast. Of all the nonsense. "What drivel! Are you actually implying that I am putting Margaret's reputation at risk by not breathing down her neck at every rout?"

"Every rout? No, of course not. But your complete absence from every event is an issue. Your presence needs to be felt, it must be shown that Margaret has someone watching out for her."

He rubbed a hand across his face, wishing he were still asleep. It was not so much that she was wrong, which she most certainly was, but it was that she was also right. He knew their world, and that a young woman needed male supervision. He knew it, and he hadn't done it.

But why was he constantly being reminded of his duty by her? He was not an errant schoolboy that needed his manners checked, and that was precisely how he felt at this moment. Yet he fought the urge to defend himself.

"Why are you staring at my feet?" he asked, genuinely perturbed.

"What?" Oddly, this seemed to discompose her, and she looked abashed. Why, he could not fathom.

"You keep staring at my feet. I thought at least you had the temerity to look a man in the eye whilst berating him."

She sighed and shook her head. Standing, she took a last look around the room, and told him she was leaving.

"Wait," he called out as she reached the door. "You have forgotten your packet." He lifted his chin at the overstuffed dossier she'd left on the floor.

"No, that is for you." She turned the knob and said over her shoulder as she walked out. "Those are all the accounts that need settling from Ashland Park."

He looked at the bulging package, dread rising in his chest. "Well, damn."

* * *

Early the next morning, Ash paid a call at his wife's house. After the humiliation at Ashland, he had, albeit belatedly, read through the marriage contract. Though he did not believe her to be the type to lie, he wanted to see the terms for himself, and there they'd been, his financial leash spelled out in black and white. If he'd learned anything from the ordeal, it was never to enter any arrangement blindly again.

Thus, he had also learned that the elegant, sparkling, and admittedly impressive new house that loomed before him was the sole property of his wife, and he'd no claim to it whatsoever. Her property remained hers, and he, well he kept the earldom afloat.

He knocked briskly at the tall black door himself, not being in possession of a footman to perform the task for him. It swung open soundlessly, and he announced himself to the butler. "The Earl of Ashland to see his wife."

Ash could have applauded the man. For a split second the butler stared at him, for who would not be astounded to find a husband, and an earl no less, knocking at what should be his own door. But he gathered himself within the moment, as cool as you like, bowing and swinging the door wide. "Of course, my lord."

The outside of the home was fairly subdued. What Ash had expected to find inside was a garish display of new wealth, an excess of trinkets and ornamentation, elaborate furnishings, and lavish accoutrements, all designed to showcase the wealth of the household to visitors. But the entryway into which he stepped was none of these things; it was elegant and uncluttered. Sunlight gleamed off the marble floors. There were flowers on a table and only one picture on the wall. The room was reasonably furnished in understated hues. He did not have time to notice more, for the butler said, "This way, my lord," and Ash followed him down the corridor.

He led him into a room of light cream walls and large windows looking out onto lush green gardens. The room was suffused with a mouthwatering aroma; the source, a sideboard mounded with food, standing in readiness against one wall. He caught a glimpse of bacon, bread, and a polished silver coffee urn before his attention turned to the center of the room, which housed a long table dressed in pristine white linen. Seated around the table, were his wife, mother and sister.

The countess read a newspaper while his mother and Margaret talked. They were at breakfast. Ash had a moment to take in the unexpected tableau of these three sharing a cozy meal before the butler announced him.

"The Earl of Ashland."

Three heads turned in unison to stare at him in varying stages of astonishment. The countess put down her paper and raised a brow, while the look his mother gave him could best be described as a squint, an expression he was sure he'd never before seen directed at himself. Only Margaret exhibited any happiness at his arrival: she squealed and jumped out of her chair to embrace him.

"Thank you, Neville. That will be all," Honora said, and then addressed the footman. "Miles, kindly prepare a plate for Lord Ashland."

Margaret released him and they took their places at the table. Ash would admit to a sense of pleasure when the footmen placed a heaping plate of food before him. His only breakfast had been a weak cup of tea, courtesy of the public house near his lodgings. He inhaled deeply, but with the three women still staring at him expectantly, refrained from picking up his fork, though his stomach protested. Instead, he folded his hands and peered back at them one by one as the smell of bacon nearly undid him.

"Oh, Ash! The season is ever so much fun and I've the most wonderful new gowns. You simply must see my darling new walking dress...." Margaret went on, chattering and smiling.

Ash was pleased at her happiness. He glanced at Mother, eating a piece of toast as she regarded him. She'd yet to say a word, making Ash suspect she just might be out of sorts with him. But no, he amended, likely it was the indignity of her surroundings. Of course, he thought, glancing around the spacious, immaculate, well-furnished room. How crass.

Next he glanced at his wife, who watched him over the rim of her tea cup. She drank slowly and deeply, her eyes conveying a spark of humor, pleased, no doubt, at his current circumstances.

"What a surprise, my lord," she said, picking up a scone and slathering it with cream. "Tell us, how have you been keeping in your quarters? I trust your situation is adequate?"

When his stomach grumbled loudly, Ash could not resist picking up his fork. "Well you might jeer, my lady, but a man needs his space. How have you three been rubbing along? Mother, I trust you are not overexerting yourself?"

Mother raised her brows. "I'd say the time for that question was over a month ago, my boy." Oh yes, there was no doubt: she was absolutely out of sorts with him. She hadn't called him *my boy* in years. Ash put down his fork with a yearning look at his plate.

"A month you have been in Town."

"Less than a month, Mother." He stopped, sensing it had not been a good idea to interrupt her. He glanced down at his plate, where the eggs were rapidly cooling. "I don't mind the dressing-down, Mother. I know I've earned it. But is it at all possible to deliver it after I've eaten my breakfast?"

"Harrumph!" Mother made a strangled sound, a mixture of shock and disgust. "Upon my word, Ashland, but you are ill-mannered."

He fought the urge to sigh and provoke her further. He really was very hungry; the sight of the food was affecting him most urgently and so casting all last attempts at civility aside, he picked up his fork again and began to eat.

Mother directed a tiny frowned at him which he, transported by the delicious mound of food before him, was able to shrug off. It seemed ages since he'd had such a decent meal. He ate at public houses, greasy fare of questionable origin, or at the club, sturdy English dishes where he was forced to endure the downright stodginess of the atmosphere.

It occurred to him that they must eat this well every morning at his wife's house.

He applied himself and cleared the plate. Finished, he sat back and returned his attention to his female relations. His mother watched him with that little frown, Margaret beamed at him and his lady wife appeared to find the entire situation vastly amusing. She wasn't doing anything so obvious as laughing, but he could decipher the tell-tale twinkle in her eye.

"Well, Mother, how do you find London? I trust you are being entertained."

Lady Celeste unbent a bit, as he suspected she would. Town and its amusements, so long denied, were bound to be her favorite topic. She proceeded to regale him with a detailed account of the balls and parties which they'd attended, Margaret interjecting with her own observations. It was, he supposed, the price he had to pay for neglecting them, so he listened, and let them talk on until they'd exhausted the topic.

Ash could not help but notice that the gleam of amusement in Honora's eye had dulled significantly.

"Society and its doings are not of interest to you?" he asked her.

"I couldn't say. I've little experience with either."

"What? Don't say you haven't been keeping Mother and Margaret company?"

"Indeed she has not," Mother interjected. "It would hardly be fitting for her to make her debut without you at her side. It will be a struggle as it is to gain her full acceptance, and we wouldn't wish to impair Margaret's chances at all. I have very high hopes for Margaret, very high hopes indeed."

This little speech was enough to kill the discussion, as even Margaret looked uncomfortable at the dowager's blatantly negative evaluation of Honora's situation.

Margaret ended up breaking the tension. "Perhaps you'd like a tour, Ash? Honora's home is beautiful and I'm sure you'll find it the most charming and modern thing! The staff are wonderful. They will undoubtedly have your belongings sorted in no time at all, and then you can properly settle in."

"My belongings?" He looked down and fiddled with the teacup, twisting it around in the saucer. "Oh, I say, that is, I wasn't planning on staying. I've only just stopped to check on all of you."

They turned to stare at him as one again. He stared back at the three-headed beast, knowing he'd angered it.

Mother's frown deepened into what was possibly the darkest look of her life. "And where, pray tell, do you think you will be keeping yourself?"

"In my own lodgings, Mother," he said firmly, intent on giving no ground. Damn if he wasn't the head of the house.

"In your own lodgings? Your *own* lodgings? And where does a man lodge other than with his wife, with his mother and sister in residence?"

"Now, Mother—"

"Need I remind you that you are the Earl of Ashland, and not some common lad about town? Need I remind you of your duty and obligation to your sister during her first and sadly delayed season?"

Honora, fortunately seeming to sense that this was only the beginning of a lengthy diatribe, finally broke her lengthy silence and said, "I daresay we should all take a moment to collect ourselves. Why don't I give you the tour, my lord?" She rose and he followed, bowing stiffly to his glaring mother before leaving the room. Honora had paused a few feet ahead of him, and leaned against the wall.

"I don't think I've ever heard your mother speak so many words at once."

"Nor have I. It's quite the harshest she's ever spoken to me."

Honora raised a brow in astonishment.

"She is usually a very gentle creature. I can't say what's gotten into her."

"Can't you?" Honora laughed in disbelief. "Then let us start the tour."

* * *

Damn him if the house wasn't one of the finest he'd ever seen, and he'd been in some of the best houses in England. Those were grand and historical and old, and this—this was new and modern and comfortable and gorgeous. Yes, gorgeous. It made his bachelor lodgings even shabbier in comparison. He began to wonder if his much-touted freedom was worth drafty windows and the constant pervasive odor of boiled meat. There were no drafts here, and the air smelled as fresh and sweet as a rose garden. Likely because there were bowls and vases filled with fresh roses everywhere. The carpet under their feet was thick and soft, muffling their footsteps. The windows were large and clean, letting bright light shine in, and everything he saw was polished and gleaming and delightful.

"I say, breakfast this morning, is that your regular cook?"

Honora glanced at him over her shoulder. "Of course."

They moved through the house, room after room grand and elegant, and eventually paused before a closed set of doors on the second floor. "The master's chambers," she said, opening both doors.

He stepped in and at the sight of the luxurious room felt a brief flash of envy for the master, until he realized that she meant him, of course. He was supposed to be the master here. It was all a man could need, spacious and smart and masculine, done up in colors of deep blue with accents of brass. An enormous bed dominated the large room, clean and no doubt dressed with the softest linens. Warm rugs lined the floor. Like the rest of the house, everything was well-ordered and inviting.

A large fireplace encircled by two cozy chairs stood to his left. To the right were two doors, one of which led to a dressing room, and the other, to one of the most wondrous things he'd ever seen.

"A bathing chamber." She flung open the door to reveal a tiled marvel, beaming at the room with open pride. "It is the most modern of its kind, see, with plumbed-in hot water—" she stepped in and turned one of the golden taps and water immediately gushed forth into the enormous white tub that graced the center of the room. Within seconds the water began to steam.

"It's very hot," she said, running a hand quickly beneath it. "Touch it."

He did, and pulled his hand back quickly from the stinging heat. She turned it off and then repeated the performance with the cold-water tap, then began opening the wooden cupboards that housed scented soaps and oils and piles of clean white towels.

Ash had been making do with a basin and ewer of tepid water. He hadn't eaten a decent meal in weeks. The master's chamber was larger than his lodgings, not to mention cleaner and directly connected to a bevy of servants to heed his needs.

He leaned over and turned the tap himself, watching with a strange satisfaction as fresh water poured copiously into the clean bathtub.

At that moment, Ash conceded. He would leave his tatty lodgings and come to live in Milady's Manor. He would have come for the food alone, or the servants, or even the soft, clean bed, but this bathing room was one of the finest things he'd ever beheld. Already he longed to sink into a tub of hot water and steep like the prosperous young lord he supposedly was. Pride be damned, he was not foolish enough to deliberately keep himself from such sumptuous surroundings.

The bathing chamber connected his room to the last room on the tour: hers. It was a surprisingly feminine room, far softer and pinker than he'd expect of her, the walls and bedcoverings a pale rose, the ceiling cream and gilt. A bedside table held stacks of books and the curtains at the tall windows were pulled back to let in a flood of light. He noted a dressing table overcrowded with bottles and jars, at odds with the neatness of the rest of the house, as though only here did she allow herself true ease.

Above the overcrowded dressing table hung a painting, a portrait of a woman dressed in clothing of the previous century. Though the clothing and the subject herself were all that was respectable, the woman stared out at the viewer with a look that somehow emitted a heavy dose of what could only be termed sensuality. Perhaps it was her full lips, or heavy eyes, but something about her expression and general demeanor emanated earthy humor and passion.

Ash was well familiar with this painting: it had hung at Ashland Park for decades, until its sale a few years ago during one of the many purges of their belongings.

He turned to Honora. "That painting used to hang in my grandfather's study," shock at seeing this familiar bit of his ancestral past here of all places turning his voice gruff.

"Did it?" she replied, though her nonchalance came across as a bit forced. He stared at her, waiting for elaboration.

When none was forthcoming, he asked, "Is there anything else?"

She turned to him, puzzled but only for a moment. "No. That is all I have from Ashland Park."

"From Ashland Park. And other houses? Have you bought up the detritus from the misfortune of other families'?"

Two bright spots appeared on her cheeks, but if he thought she would be ashamed, he was mistaken. "Aristocratic pride that will prevent a man from doing honest work to save his own skin is hardly misfortune."

Because he was tired of arguing and even more disinclined to receive another lecture on the failures of his class, he chose not to respond. He sat down instead, at the little stool before her vanity table, and focused his whirling thoughts on how to announce his intention to take up residence while maintaining some degree of dignity. Why, he could be soaking in that bathing tub this very night. Damn the painting and all it represented.

She took a seat as well, perching on the end of her bed. After all of the distractions with the breakfast and his mother and the tour of the house, he hadn't actually gotten a proper look at her, and now that he did, found her looking quite well indeed. Though he'd decided she was too thin for his taste, he would admit that she possessed a favorable, well-proportioned figure, and was elegant in her blue gown. Her dark hair highlighted her creamy skin, and she regarded him with large, pretty eyes.

"You look very well today," he blurted. She frowned in response. Clearly he'd no need to regret voicing his opinion, she obviously did not believe him. He supposed he'd be skeptical in her place as well.

"Have you looked at the accounts I left you?" she asked.

"I've hardly had time, you only gave them to me yesterday."

She raised a brow, a habit of hers, he was coming to learn. "You had all night."

"All night?" He laughed. "I do not spend my nights at home, reading over accounts." He'd meant to sound dismissive, but his words sounded foolish, even to himself. Her mouth twisted at the corner, and for the second time in as many days, he felt himself judged and found lacking. Worse yet, he wasn't sure if that judgement was hers or his own.

Was this how he wanted to live, with silent assessment and raised eyebrows? Damnation. He thought of the congested lodgings and then of the spacious chamber and glorious bathing room next door and swallowed his misgivings.

"I have reconsidered," he said magnanimously. "I will bring my belongings from the lodgings and take up residence here. Margaret and Mother would certainly benefit from my presence in the house, and I daresay I may provide some service as an escort to you."

"Oh?" she scoffed. "How very good of you."

"Isn't it?" He was on his feet before he knew it, standing before her in a few short steps. He stood over her so that she had to tip her head up to look at him, a motion that caused her to lean back and brace herself upon the bed. He leaned in closer still.

"I find I like the notion of nightly proximity to my wife. So much better than a cold, empty bed."

"Has your bed been empty?" Her large dark eyes watched him, unblinking. Damn her constant composure.

He bent down and took her mouth with his, capturing her chin between two fingers. He pressed his tongue into her mouth, expecting at any moment to be pushed off in a flurry of indignation. Instead she opened for him with a soft sound, as though she liked it. She'd no qualm with meeting his tongue with her own, so sweetly hot and wet.

He recalled how she'd looked at him, watched his mouth, his bare feet, and realization struck. He pulled back, seeing the confirmation in her flushed face and swollen lips. Her chest rose in rapid breaths. His grip on her chin tightened and he smiled slowly, desire and a sense of victory unfurling within him.

"So you do want me." It was the first time he'd felt he'd an advantage with her, and he found he liked the concept that there was something more than a title that she wanted from him.

She blinked up at him and he could see the denial forming on her lips. Rather than let it surface, he kissed her again, kissed her quiet until she melted against him once more, no longer capable of denying anything.

* * *

Having wasted the better part of her morning with touring her own house, Honora hurried to her study, and to the mountain of work that required her attention there. There were issues at the Botham offices, questions from the architect at Ashland, and many requests from charities pleading for her help. Not least, she wanted a moment to herself, away from Ash and the distraction of his charming face.

She needed to focus; the vast Botham interests needed a strong captain at the helm, one whose attention never flagged. But *la*, he was so handsome, a divinity set down in her house, and when he gazed at her with those blue eyes, she wanted to gaze back and believe him when he said she looked well. To hear him compliment her... It was the highest, and perhaps only compliment he'd ever paid her. And his mouth on hers...

Fool's games. She could hear Granny now, as if the woman stood in the room, speaking directly into her ear. Fool's games to let his looks distract her, to let the work accumulate, to lose sight of her goals. From her earliest days she'd been taught never to neglect the business. She'd spent many a night with Granny working, taking care of one urgency or another, not sleeping, not eating, not socializing.

But she was a countess now, a wife, and had duties that Granny perhaps could not have envisioned. The role entailed socializing, entering the echelons that the title had brought her. Her stomach lurched at the thought.

And of course there were her wifely responsibilities, the thought of which caused an altogether different kind of jolt, one that flared as an aching heat low in her abdomen and travelled down between her legs. She recalled the amazement in his eyes earlier, when he'd realized she wanted him. How shocked he would be to learn the true depths of her desire for him: that she'd never not wanted him, had craved him from the very beginning.

She expelled a shaky breath and did her utmost to shift her focus away from Ashland and to her work, but the ache between her legs lingered, and she could not dislodge him from her thoughts completely.

CHAPTER NINE

I f Honora feared further disruption of her household routine by her husband's presence, she need not have been concerned. On his first evening there they ate their supper *à deux*, the dowager and Margaret having gone out to their own evening engagement with close friends. Ash was thoroughly enamored of the food, eating with a hitherto unforeseen gusto. She spent most of her meal watching him eat, amazed at the unguarded joy on his face. When they adjourned to the drawing room, he took a seat close to the fire, though the air was hardly chilled, and promptly fell asleep, hands folded across his middle. It was where Honora left him two hours later, when she went up to seek her own bed.

The rest of the week continued much the same. She was rather astonished at his domesticity, having assumed he would wish to continue the manly pursuits he'd held so dear whilst at the bachelor lodgings, activities which she could only guess at. Instead he seemed as tame and content as a housecat, finding pleasure simply in being well-fed and warm.

And yet he intruded upon her thoughts, the mere knowledge of his physical presence elsewhere in the house causing her usual fierce concentration to falter, while simultaneously keeping her from removing herself to her offices.

On the day that they would attend their first ball together, Ash came to her study. She marveled at his easy elegance; he took no special care in his appearance, and yet when he walked into the room her breath froze in her throat at the sight of him. It hardly seemed fair.

He looked around, taking in the shelves full of books, a stack of newspapers on a side table, her enormous desk covered in ledgers and folios and various papers. Finally he rested his gaze upon her and smiled in that crooked way he had, one corner of his mouth lifting higher than the other. Honora schooled her features, struggling not to show any reaction to his presence.

"Tell me you aren't hiding." He leaned over her desk.

"Hiding?" she asked, puzzled, still dazzled by that grin.

"Tonight? The ball? Your debut as Countess of Ashland?" He picked up a paper weight and jiggled it in the palm of his hand. "What on earth is this?"

"It's raw copper. From one of our Cornish mines."

He shrugged and set down the green-tarnished rock, then took a seat at one of the two chairs before her desk. "Shouldn't you be primping or..." he waved a hand in the air before his face to indicate the vagaries of female grooming.

"I beg your pardon?" Honora surreptitiously ran a hand over her hair. It felt well in place and as far as she knew, she had no visible stains on her person.

His brow creased in a tiny frown. "Don't women need hours to prepare for this sort of thing? Seems Mother and Margaret started preparing yesterday."

Honora suppressed a sigh. Mother and Margaret were fortunate enough to have no other obligations other than primping and preparing. She kept her silence, having reached a point where she was tired of hearing the refrain from herself.

"I'll go up in a while to bathe and ready myself. It's hardly strenuous," she said drily.

Ash looked up at her through his lashes, a look she couldn't read but which nevertheless made her blood warm. He smiled a slow knowing grin and Honora's heart soared at the sensation that he was smiling *at her*, that the look of delight on his face was for her and her alone.

"Honora," he breathed, and held her gaze. Honora's mouth went dry, her palms grew damp and she leaned slightly forward. "I do not scruple to tell you that the bathing chamber is one of the finest things I have ever seen in my life. I could soak for days. You are brilliant."

He would, of course, compliment her on the bathing facilities. Her heart sank a little to its normal plateau. She smiled grimly down at the splotchy document before her, silently chiding herself for acting like a smitten schoolgirl.

The dowager and Margaret, true to form, were thrilled at the prospect of the evening's festivities and, whatever they may have felt, demonstrated no misgivings about securing Honora's elusive standing in society.

Honora did her part, bathed and dressed and draped herself in jewels rare enough to proclaim her status, and modest enough to convey a proper lack of pretention, lest anyone find her more grasping than they already did. She was the first female downstairs, met at the bottom of the staircase by her husband, effortlessly handsome in his evening attire. "Enchanting," he greeted her, and graciously pressed a kiss to the back of her gloved hand. And she clung to it, though it was only politeness.

He paid similar compliments to his mother and sister when they finally descended. He paused near the dowager.

"But Mother, what is this?" he asked, indicating the brilliant necklace adorning her neck. "And Margaret, you, too? What on earth?"

"Honora was kind enough to loan them to us," Margaret replied breathlessly, resting a gloved hand on the diamond pendant. "Aren't they stunning, Ash? I vow I feel like a princess!"

He looked at her with such warm surprise that Honora didn't know whether to be overjoyed or offended. But the growing anxiety over the night ahead brought a spark of irritation and she snapped, "They can hardly go without jewels, as virtually all of their own have been sold off. At least the respectable ones."

The warmth in his gaze abruptly faded. He inclined his head and they made their way to the carriage in silence.

"You look very well tonight, Honora," the dowager said as they settled into their seats, startling Honora with the unexpected compliment. "You are fortunate not to be overly pretty. I fear there will be a great deal of curiosity about you, and beauty can generate jealousy, you know."

"Evidently I do not," Honora muttered under her breath. Ash's head came round and he stared at her, but she held his gaze until he looked away.

"Indeed, indeed. I had many a disagreeable experience during my own youth, rivals who were envious of my fine looks and I will tell you it is very unpleasant. Very unpleasant."

Honora withstood the temptation to roll her eyes, and in no time they had achieved their destination. She took a deep breath and exited the carriage.

* * *

They passed through the hot and crowded ballroom slowly, making their way through greetings and introductions of names and faces too numerous to recall. Ashland was certainly well-known, and many people feigned an interest in making her acquaintance. They spoke to her in that sophisticated way they had, silent condescension under a veneer of refinement that exhausted her. But this was their world, the one to which she'd aspired, so she kept her head high and a cool smile on her lips as their eyes raked her over and then met with arch looks over her shoulder, devilishly amused at the tradeswoman that had dared dress up as a countess.

When Ashland finally took her to the dance floor, she breathed a sigh of relief, so glad to be away from the creatures that had thronged around them.

"It might help if you were a bit warmer," he said, gazing over her shoulder as they began to move to the music.

"I beg your pardon?"

"You're very unwelcoming in your demeanor. I think you'd have better luck at engaging with others if you weren't radiating displeasure."

They twirled.

Honora felt a hot flush creep up her neck, unwelcome anger and defensiveness. "You don't know what you're talking about."

"I've watched you since we got here, barely uttering a word and literally looking down your nose at the ladies who've approached you. Judging their lack of personal merit?"

Honora inhaled. "How dare you!"

He looked down at her, his eyes a dark blue challenge in the candlelight. "Do you find them inferior?"

Honora could not speak for several minutes, debating how much and what to say, until finally, "Did you know that I had a debut?"

He raised a brow, clearly uninterested.

"It was ten years ago. My grandmother wrangled a sponsor for me, intent on presenting me to better society." He guided them through the dancing throng with surety, nodding at someone behind her. The warmth of his palm at her waist did nothing to dispel the coolness of his judgement.

"As you can well imagine, it was a disaster. There was no one at the time willing to overlook the inferiority of my background to befriend me, let alone marry me. After two months Granny allowed me to withdraw. I am not a complete stranger to these ladies tonight; many of them must remember me very well from that catastrophe. They are still all too happy to pick me apart."

His mouth clamped down and they swirled in silence. She was not sure if she'd offended him or further humiliated herself; she did not care. Some part of her had wanted to see his indignation on her behalf and now she was left fighting a stupid disappointment at being chastised instead.

Only as the dance was coming to a close did he lean down and say directly into her ear, "But you are the Countess of Ashland now, not Miss Botham of nowhere. Do not let them forget it."

He turned as the music died, and walked away.

* * *

It did not take him above fifteen minutes to feel the veriest scoundrel for abandoning her. He'd fully intended to make his way to a game or two of cards, but her words began to replay in his mind, and he understood the expression on her face was one of panic, and not the detached condescension he'd initially assumed. He turned back into the teeming ballroom with a muttered curse, and tried to make his way back to her, impeded by the crush of bodies and those who stopped him to for a word or a greeting.

When at last he spotted her, she stood alone, isolated in the press of people, a tiny island of solitude, her back rigid, her face carefully wiped of any emotion. He saw a woman behind her rake her gaze over her gown, and then turn with a comment to her twittering friends.

He shoved his way through them, not bothering with apologies, hoping he might crush a toe or two.

"There you are," he breathed with relief, placing a hand possessively at her waist. She turned at the sound of his voice, the look of surprise on her face chastising him more than any reproach could. "Let us find some fresh air." He guided her out of the ballroom and onto a quiet terrace, whereupon she immediately stepped from his grasp in an admirable swirl of skirts. She moved to the stone balustrade and rested her hands upon it, looking every inch the noble potentate surveying her domain. Ash laughed.

"I am glad you are amused."

"Oh, not so much amused as pleased to see the steel back in your spine." He moved next to her and looked out over the darkened garden. The music and sounds of the ball poured out of the open doors, though the air outside was blessedly fresher. "I didn't know what to make of you when you had that ossified look on your face."

She made a little sound, like a sigh of agreement. "I am not at my best in this environment."

He leaned on the balustrade to look at her, though her features were obscured by the shadows. "Let me fetch you some champagne." She stopped him with a touch on the arm.

"No. Please. I'd rather just enjoy the air for a moment." She retracted her hand and turned away, staring out at the murky shrubbery and Ash did as she asked, waiting in silence, though he wanted to bring her champagne and make her merry enough to overlook his bad manners.

A heady aroma rose from the dark garden, enveloping the terrace in its fragrance. Above, the moon shone dimly, waxing through heavy clouds.

By God, it was positively romantic.

How many times had he fruitlessly conspired to maneuver a woman thus, alone onto a shadowy and perfumed terrace? Now he had done it and with a woman that was his lawful wife, no less, with no chance of discovery by a fuming chaperone. Why, he could lean over and kiss her senseless and the most he could be accused of was bad taste at such a vulgar display.

It was an appealing notion. He studied her profile, the stubborn tilt to her jaw that he'd started to become familiar with. Her ivory-hued skin glowed rather prettily in the moonlight; he imagined it must feel as soft as velvet.

He leaned in a bit, until he was close enough that the perfume of her body overpowered the flowery air. He angled his head—

"It's not that I care for their opinion." Her voice startled him into taking a step back. It was not too dark to see her hands clench on the stone railing. "I place a far higher value on my opinion of myself. It is only the pretense that galls me."

Ash took a deep breath and raked a hand through his hair, trying to remember exactly how much he'd had to drink. He was acting like a fool, caught up in flowers and moonlight. "Pretense?"

She nodded at him. "The charade of good manners. It would all be much easier if I could simply speak my mind."

He could not help but laugh again, for it was a delightfully amusing notion. He felt a bit better to hear a soft giggle from her in response.

"You are a countess. You could probably say anything you like."

"Oh? I'm afraid that is a man's purview. Women, regardless of rank, are held to a different standard. Women are not to speak directly. No, a woman must speak around her thoughts, to convey her opinion in the most agreeable and circuitous fashion as possible."

"And it galls you that you cannot find a pretty way to say 'Go to the devil'?"

She turned to him, a denial obviously at the tip of her tongue. She paused instead, and shrugged.

"It does not make for a pleasant evening," he finished for her, watching her as she turned away to contemplate the shadows. It wasn't much of a pleasant evening for him, either. Honora's tension had affected him, and he wasn't feeling particularly good at how he'd handled himself thus far. He liked to believe himself more of a gentleman than his actions tonight had demonstrated.

They stared out at the shadowy foliage in silence made easy by the insulating darkness. The ball carried on behind them. But before them was the open night, spread out for the taking. Ash was struck by a brilliant idea. "Let us go."

"I am not yet ready to return to the ball."

"No." He took her arm and turned her toward him. "Let us go from here."

"Leave the ball, you mean?" She was already shaking her head.

"Why should we not?"

"We've only been here a short while. Your mother and Margaret—"

"Are likely having a merry time. We shan't disturb them. Come! It's not far to home, we can walk and leave the carriage."

In the fractured light he could make out her uncertain expression, hesitation mixed with longing.

"We have the privilege of making our own rules," he urged, abruptly wanting to be gone himself. "It's a dull party anyway." Which was true. Also true, he'd spotted Lady Amelia Bates across the ballroom earlier, a frothy confection of ruffle and bows who'd made no effort at hiding the beckoning look in her eye as their gazes had met. She'd traced her fan across that abundant cleavage as she'd smiled at him, her new husband nowhere in sight. Ash thought it best if he avoided encountering her.

It took a moment but Honora finally nodded and smiled, a soft beam of acceptance that pleased him no end.

He found a footman to retrieve Honora's cloak and relay the news of their departure to his mother. When she pointed out that her flimsy silk slippers would hardly withstand walking home, he managed to find a maid who traded her sturdy work boots for the slippers and a coin, happy with the bargain. He bent down before his wife and laced the boots himself as she braced herself against his shoulder, her gown and the soft scent of soap drifting around him.

They circumvented the crowd and left by a side door, adding a shade of defiance to their departure, laughing as the Smith-Covington's home retreated behind them.

* * *

"I can in all honesty say I've never left a party in such a fashion," Honora said as they walked through the gaslit streets. There were few people about at the late hour, but with her arm snugly entwined with Ashland's, she felt safe and carefree. "Wearing the maid's shoes." She shook her head in wonder and peered down at the sturdy boots.

"Better than the footman's waistcoat," Ash answered drily.

Honora laughed at the image, and then gasped and looked up at him, belatedly alarmed. "Oh, your mother will be livid when she learns we've left!"

"I instructed the butler to inform her of our departure one hour hence and not a minute sooner." The left corner of his mouth quirked up.

"You've done this before."

He shrugged. "Here and there. All due respect to Mother, but we've different ideas of entertainment.

Honestly, I've never understood the crushing desire to attend these things. It's the same people in different clothes. At any rate, Mother's likely to blame you for our premature departure, anyway."

"Me? Whatever for?"

"I also instructed the butler to tell her you were ill."

Honora stopped in her tracks and stared at him.

"Look, that's how it works." He looked down at her, the corner of his mouth winding upward. "That's the sacrifice on your end. If she thought I initiated the departure she'd be all manner of suspicious. This way, we have a plausible excuse. I'd say we've got two more uses at most before we've got to think up another scheme."

Honora realized he was both serious and not, and laughed at the absurdity. "I'll never have to attend another ball again. I can simply walk in and walk right out."

"Of course you can. Remember what I said: You're a countess now, you can make your own rules. And if one of those is only a brief appearance at social events, then so be it. You've got to get used to it."

"Your mother believes I should establish myself in the position—"

"Listen." Ash stepped closer to her and took her by the shoulders, the imprint of his fingers clear even through the velvet of her spencer jacket. The nearby street lamp illuminated his face perfectly and Honora's breath froze in her chest, overcome, again, by his looks and closeness. "Allow me to be blunt. They're not likely to ever fully accept you, not the way my mother wants. Too many of them are too penniless to ever look kindly on new money. Not," he hurried on, seeing the mutinous look on her face, "that I agree. But it's better to see things as they are and not languish in fantasy."

Honora was stunned into silence. It wasn't the notion that surprised her as much at his astuteness. The mix of emotions must have shown on her face, for he looked at her kindly.

"I'm not as dim as you thought," he added in a teasing, accusatory tone.

She paused for a moment. "No. No, you are not."

That earned her a laugh, and he turned and they continued walking.

It was an agreeable evening, fresh and cool, the atmosphere on the street far preferable to that of the recently exited ballroom. She liked the solid feel of him beside her, the warmth and scent of him ameliorating her earlier displeasure from the ball, the muscles of his forearm strong beneath her hand. She tried to imagine herself sharing his carefree disposition, blithely going into the night with no thought of deserted responsibilities.

"What of Margaret?" Honora asked after a while. "Doesn't she need our presence?"

"For all anyone knows I'm still at that ball, looming protectively, albeit in some other room. In that crowd it's impossible to tell. And if our joint absence is noticed, it will only be assumed that we've disappeared for a tryst." He wiggled his eyebrows lecherously.

It was a joke, but one that sent a rush of heat through Honora's abdomen, heat that shot through the rest of her, utterly discomfiting her. *A tryst.* She wished it were true. "I would so dislike to disappoint her," she managed to say, telling herself he could not possibly guess at the lustful forces moving through her, earnestly trying to keep her thoughts on Margaret's well-being.

"You're married to me now, so you'll have to learn how to dodge responsibility when you can." He patted her hand where it rested on his arm. "Margaret will be fine. Mother will find her a perfect husband, she'll make cherub-faced grandchildren and turn into a proper plump matron."

Honora wished she shared his careless confidence, but experience, and Granny, had taught her that life seldom turned out for the best simply because one assumed it would. Perhaps circumstances were different for the Earl of Ashland. Mayhap after generations of good breeding the upper classes had sufficiently mastered the whims of life and eliminated uncertainty and insecurity.

They walked on, her arm snug in his, his flesh warm under hers, and she tried to cast aside thoughts of Margaret and the upper classes. Anyone looking at them would take them for a contented couple, making their way lazily home under the stars and moon, sweet-talking in the shadows between streetlamps. For a moment Honora allowed herself to bask in the illusion, let herself feel that theirs was a marriage in truth. Illusions, she found, were well and good as long as one recognized them for what they were and did not slip into mistaking them for reality.

In reality she was in a mismatched marriage of convenience with a devilishly charming and attractive man. Under normal circumstances, she would not allow herself to function outside of that fact. But for this one moonlit walk, she would indulge the little-visited and spectacularly fantastical portion of her brain and pretend that she was a woman being escorted home on the arm of the man who loved her. She gave his arm a tentative squeeze, nothing he was likely to feel, and moved closer to him.

CHAPTER TEN

Once home, they retired to their separate chambers, whereupon Ash decided that a bath was in order. Truthfully, he found such pleasure in the bathing chamber that he bathed nearly every day for the sheer enjoyment of it; the wonder of the room turned the simple chore into an indulgence. He unwound his cravat and tossed it onto the table, and began removing his jacket. He'd a proper valet now, an efficient man called Madden, but he'd dismissed him to bed, wanting a bit of solitude.

He liked the silence of his room. He liked his plush surroundings, his stately bed, his orderly belongings. He loved the cook and the modern bathing room and the lack of drafts and mice. He loved his velvet dressing gown and soft slippers, and the sense of finally having a stable roof over their heads.

He sat down to tug off his boots, reflecting on the unexpected turn of the past evening and precisely how Honora was not the rigid and humorless being he'd imagined her to be. Well, she was rigid and humorless, but it turned out to be only a part of her personality and not the entirety of it. Her uncertainty tonight had revealed a vulnerability he hadn't imagined she possessed, though she'd likely choke to hear it. And she'd been a remarkably good sport about the silly way they'd escaped the ball. She'd been... well, she'd been damn good fun, unable to hide her delight at the manner in which they'd vanished from the ball.

Tonight, he realized with a swell of satisfaction, was the first time he'd ever been of service to her. The notion that such a thing mattered to him made him pause, a boot hanging from one hand.

In their marriage, which was the sum total of their entire relationship, he'd been the recipient of Honora's largesse: her money, her considerable management skills, and yes, even her drive and ambition. All of these things had benefited Ashland the estate and Ashland the man. He sat back and she managed everything.

It wasn't a pretty realization.

Only tonight, she'd needed him. She'd been virtually helpless in that ballroom until he'd taken matters into his own hands and led her away.

But only because she'd let him.

He frowned at that thought, and tossed the boot aside. It thumped onto the carpet. He stood, pulling out his shirttails from his trousers as he walked to the bathing room door. It was only as he put his hand on the knob that the sounds pierced his thoughts, soft murmuring of voices and the splash of water. He cracked the door to peer inside; Honora was inside with her maid, preparing for her bath. A cloud of lilac soap-scented steam rolled off the gushing water. The room glowed with the light of candles and wall sconces.

He meant to go, but just before he could turn away, the maid stepped behind Honora and lifted the pink silken wrapper from her shoulders, leaving her clad in white corset and stockings. With the perfect view afforded by the gap in the door, he watched as Honora unfastened her bracelet, and raised a foot onto a little stool. The maid knelt before her, and began unfastening her shoe, the sturdy boot she'd left the ball in. It should have been a ridiculous contrast, that scuffed and utilitarian black shoe against the refined white silk of her undergarments and skin; instead, it was deeply arousing.

Once the boots were off, Honora raised her skirts and the maid's hands moved to the exposed stocking, rolling it down with practiced ease from mid-thigh and over the arch of a dainty foot. Once complete, she repeated the process on the other leg.

Ash was absolutely frozen in place, his hand tight on the doorknob. A strange pounding sounded in his ears and he realized it was his heartbeat, which originated somewhere deep in his balls. He was rock hard. He should turn, and go. He should.

But the maid stood again, and moved to relieve Honora of her corset. Free of this constraining garment, Honora ran her hands over her torso, massaging the constrained flesh, absentmindedly rubbing her breasts. He could easily see her pink nipples through the thin chemise.

As the maid busied herself with putting away the corset, Honora reached down and lifted the chemise over her head by the hem, and in one smooth movement was completely unclothed.

Ash's breath caught in his throat. It was wicked, peeking at her through the door, naked, and though he knew he should move away he had no intention of doing so, enthralled by the very wickedness.

He took the opportunity to study her from head to toe.

She stood in profile to him, looking into the distance, clearly lost in her own thoughts. Her breasts were small and pert, tipping upward to the peak of her pink nipple, taut and full at the kiss of air. Her ribcage tapered down to a small waist, and then flared out gently over softly curved hips. Near the apex of her thighs he glimpsed the shadow of dark hair. She was tall and lean, finely formed and perfectly proportioned. And while Ash typically preferred his women rounder and softer, there was a delicacy to Honora, long, graceful bones that made her fragile and beautiful at once.

Such delicacy ended at a surprisingly round derriere. It curved out superbly from her slim waist, and Ash was suddenly overcome with the image of taking her from behind, holding her by the rump as he pushed into her.

He stifled a groan. How? How had he never noticed? God, he'd bedded her more than once.

And he'd been foxed every time, he realized. Inept and unobservant.

The maid then helped her into the bath. Honora leaned back against the large bathing tub, resting her head with a sigh of contentment. Now, now he should leave, and he would have, but just at that moment she stretched, arching her back so that the tips of her sweet breasts thrust through the surface of the water, and he was done for, willfully frozen in place.

After a quiet moment, the maid moved back into sight. She soaped a cloth, and began washing her mistress, who dutifully moved back and forth, lifting first her arms, then her legs out of the water to be washed by the attentive servant.

It was at this point that Ash's hand moved to the fastening of his trousers. They were open in a second, and he took his cock into his tight fist.

The maid knelt at the side of the tub. Honora moved forward so she could apply the soapy cloth to her torso. The maid rubbed it over her collarbone, her ribcage and straight over her puckered nipples and breasts. Honora's eyes stayed closed the entire time as she submitted to the matter-of-fact ministrations of her servant.

Ash's hand moved faster.

After the washing was done—had it gone into any more detail he would have likely expired on the spot—Honora stood and the maid began rinsing her. The fresh water cascaded down her supple body, rinsing away the trails of soap in erotic glory. He watched one particular stream make its way to the thatch of hair between her legs, and imagined his lips following the same course.

He would come at any moment, but he prolonged the release, stilling the movements of his hand to relish the show before him.

It was when Honora stepped from the bath, putting her hand daintily in her maid's, and stood in meek obedience as the maid took the towel and began drying her mistress that he exploded. Ash did not tear his eyes away as the maid moved the towel over Honora's bare skin, over her shoulders to her breasts to her abdomen. Ash came and came as the maid knelt before her and rubbed her long legs, biting his free hand to keep from calling out.

He was still coming as Honora pulled the pins and freed her hair, still coming as she ran her fingers over her scalp, flipped her head upside down, and pointed her perfect, round, fascinating, derriere straight at him.

* * *

Honora considered taking breakfast in her room, since she'd supposedly been indisposed the night before, but decided that she would not be cowed in her own home and went down to enjoy her meal. As it was, she need not have worried; the breakfast room stood empty.

She'd harbored some spark of anticipation at seeing Ashland, realizing it only upon spotting his empty chair. Admonishing herself to embrace the solitude while she could, she settled down to her meal and newspaper. This was the first morning she'd had the room to herself since she'd returned to London. For years she'd breakfasted in this room alone without a second thought, yet now the silence grew very noticeable within minutes. In no time, she had grown used to the chatty presence of the others, in what had become the most relaxed portion of the day between the four occupants of the house. Why, they had fallen into a routine.

She looked around and wished she had someone with whom to share the astonishing piece of news. Neville chose that moment to look in, raising his brows in inquiry, but she did not think the butler would much care for her revelation.

And then Margaret came in. Only, Honora did not know how to share such profound revelations with the younger woman, so they stuck to pleasantries and a general overview of last night's ball.

"Mother was concerned you'd taken ill, but I say you look well this morning, Honora. Actually,"

Margaret lowered her voice to a whisper and peered over her shoulder at the door, "she's persuaded your spell last night has more to do with a *delicate condition,* and that perhaps you overexerted yourself."

Honora nearly spit out her coffee. "Delicate condition?" she repeated before she could stop herself.

Margaret's eyes widened. "You know, when a woman—"

"Yes! I know. Of course, I know. Only, I am not, that is to say, it is not—"

"Oh, Honora! You've no need to discuss it with me. I'm sure it's only natural and wonderful, and who wouldn't want their very own precious baby? Besides, Mother thinks me far more ignorant of the world than I am."

This was somewhat alarming news to Honora. "Margaret, I am seeing a new side to you this morning." A new side revealed, perhaps, only in the unusual absence of her mother or brother. Another realization: it was the first time she had been alone with Margaret. What an illuminating morning.

To steer the conversation away from delicate conditions, she asked how Margaret's season was proceeding, and received an effusive earful of details. "I imagine you have made many friends, many young ladies such as yourself?" Honora asked as she buttered some bread. For a moment Margaret's good-natured expression seemed to dim.

"Most of the young ladies have known each other for years, since childhood really, whereas I've been at Ashland my entire life. And I think, perhaps, it's rather hard to get to know a group of people who seem to be content with the friends they already have. Oh, but it's so wonderful! And London is so grand!"

Something in her tone sounded a bit forced. Honora wondered if matters weren't quite as 'grand' as Margaret made them out to be.

"Good morning."

Margaret and Honora turned their heads to look at Ash, who'd stopped in the doorway. He cast a glum look over them and then to the sideboard, as though faced with an impossibly difficult task.

"Well, come in. Why are you just standing in the doorway?" Margaret asked, frowning in puzzlement.

"Indeed," Honora added with a smile. "It's no secret you adore Cook's meals."

He looked at her and away, sending a plummeting sensation through Honora as she instantly realized the easy companionship of last night was inexplicably gone.

He nodded and deigned to enter the room, heading straight for the buffet, but lacking his usual enthusiasm. The stiff motions as he loaded his plate were at odds with the man who normally clapped his hands together in gleeful anticipation at the sight of the breakfast offerings.

Honora turned her attentions back to Margaret. A weighty sensation of foolishness had erased her appetite. She kept her gaze away from him as he took his seat beside her.

"Ash, dear," Margaret said with a sly glance at her brother, "I was just telling Honora that your unexpected departure last night has mother convinced you've started an heir."

Ash choked, sputtering so badly that Honora surged to her feet. Before she could reach his side he overcame his fit, coughing into a napkin. His face had gone beet red.

"Margaret!" he barked. "I will thank you to keep such comments to yourself." He glanced quickly at Honora and away, his mouth such a tight line that she'd think him embarrassed, if she didn't know better.

"Really, Ash! When did you become so missish?" Margaret asked with a laugh that earned her a glare. "It is a perfectly normal consequence to marriage!"

"Margaret!" He banged his hand on the table, rattling the silver and wiping Margaret's grin from her face.

Mortification rolled through Honora. His reaction made his feelings on having a child with her very clear. Of course. Her deepest desire was repugnant to him, just as the notion of marrying her had been. A child was probably unwelcome; it was probably why he never came to her bed.

She was still standing. With extreme care she placed her napkin on the table and turned to go, unwilling for these people to read any reaction on her face.

"Honora!" Margaret called after her.

"Margaret, enough!" Ash cut his sister off.

Honora left the room without another word.

And was astounded when Ash followed her out of it.

"Wait!" he called, though she hadn't gone very far, was in fact standing just outside the door.

He stopped short, evidently having anticipated she would have run farther off. Chasing after her seemed to have been his sole goal for jumping from the table; he stared at her mutely.

Honora tilted her head, prepared to wait. She wondered did other newly-wedded couples experience this ongoing stage of awkwardness and confusion in their dealings with one another. She recalled Charlotte and Sir William and did not think so.

Ash brushed his hand through his dark hair, a gesture so raffishly appealing that she suspected he well knew its effects.

"Yes?" She sighed in defeat, exasperated by the power his allure had over her. Even now, when she resolved to resist him, she found herself mesmerized by the curve of his jaw, the slope where it met his ear, the strong shape of his chin and the charm of his mouth above it.

"We should," he stopped, mouth quirking, and when he spoke again she had the feeling he wasn't saying what he'd originally intended to. "We should ride this afternoon in the park. It would be beneficial, I believe. After last night."

He kept his gaze trained in the vicinity of her chin. "Last night was..." He raised his eyes to hers, looking positively tormented.

She frowned, wondering if he'd been drinking, out of patience with the entire interaction. "Why on earth are you so troubled over asking me to ride in the park? You needn't go anywhere with me, if it's so bothersome to you!"

At this he appeared to snap out of his peculiar reverie. He smiled, that usual enticing smile which she ought to guard against, but instead pierced right through her and made her realize, for the thousandth or millionth time, how spectacularly handsome he was. Really, the constant realization was becoming tiresome.

"Last night was wonderful. I look forward to this afternoon." He grinned and returned to the breakfast room, leaving her gaping after him.

* * *

Last night had been a revelation. He'd never imagined the sight of his wife in her glory could so flood him with desire. Oh, to have seen all of that creamy white skin, the rosy nipples and that perfectly shaped backside; well, he'd gotten a far better bargain than he'd realized, and he wasn't going to waste any more time missing out. It was what spouses did, conjugal relations being the foundation of the institution of marriage and all that.

True, it had taken all of last night and the better part of the morning to accustom himself to the feeling of desire that had overtaken him. With Honora it was all tied up in the dynamic of their marriage and feelings of inferiority over the entire matter, feelings which he was convinced were best left unexplored.

But once the shock had worn off he'd been more than thrilled at the notion of this enticing, creamy skinned, long-legged creature a mere doorway away from his bed. He imagined those long legs wrapped tightly around him and smiled.

It was how he spent his entire afternoon. He took her out in the barouche, sitting too close to her and draping an arm over the seat behind her, ignoring the eyebrows that were raised his way. She tried to lean forward, visibly puzzled by his behavior, but short of hurling herself from the bench could only go so far.

At one point her lilac soap rose up in a cloud, assaulting him with the memories of the show he'd witnessed last night, and he grew instantly hard. He tortured and treated himself by imagining all the things they'd do in bed that night, and resumed smiling, not caring that he looked like a smirking fool to all the fashionable world.

* * *

Honora looked up from the letter she was writing to find Ash watching her. She shot him an arch look that left him unfazed. His gaze lingered, broody and unwavering. With a sigh of exasperation, she put her pen down. "Why do you stare?" she asked, puzzled and impatient.

Her voice seemed to move him from his trance. He shook his head, and looked to the window behind her. "Just lost in thought," he muttered, and shifted in his chair to cross his legs.

For some reason he'd followed her into the drawing room after dinner and here they'd sat for an hour with nary a word exchanged between them. Honora played at penning a letter, but in reality her attention was all on Ash, or rather on his gaze, resting on her with palpable frequency. Occasionally his fingers tapped out a staccato cadence against the arm of his chair. She would look up and he would glance away. She'd the oddest sensation he was waiting for something.

Shrugging off his response, she turned back to her letter and after another fruitless quarter hour, excused herself to bed.

It startled her when some time later, long after she'd gotten into bed with a book, he opened the door connecting their rooms. He sauntered in without a pardon, stopping at the sight of her sitting under the bedclothes.

Honora's hand flew reflexively to her eyeglasses. Defensive irritation immediately swelled within her, that all-too-familiar feeling that proximity with him seemed to generate with increasing regularity. With the constant possibility that his remarks would be dismissive or cutting, wariness was always close to the surface. Alas, realizing the fact did nothing to ameliorate it. She stubbornly forced her hand down, leaving the eyeglasses in place.

"Yes," she sighed, putting her book face down on the blanket. "I am reading a book, and before you can cleverly comment, I am wearing spectacles to do it."

Spectacles. Very likely the biggest secret she'd kept from him: her reliance on a pair of round, metal, devilishly unfashionable reading glasses. It was a silly vanity, hiding it from him, one in all honesty she'd have gladly continued, given the choice. She folded her hands tightly on the quilt, fighting the urge to remove the eyeglasses.

Ash inclined his head, watching her, the corner of his mouth quirking up. "They are rather...studious. But you do not wear them when you work?"

"I do not. They help me at the end of the day, when my eyes are tired." She heard herself, how prim and brisk she sounded, and a sense of resentment rose within her that she did not know how to sound otherwise.

He had removed his jacket and cravat, his waistcoat hung open. At the base of his throat lay a shadowy hollow of bare skin which caught her attention. It was only a bit of skin, really, but far more than she usually had the opportunity to glimpse, and she stared at it, instantly imagining pressing her lips there.

It made her blush, like a fool. She looked away, anywhere but at him. But the heat had risen in her and would not so easily fade.

He stepped a bit closer to the bed.

"Do you read every night?"

"When I am able. If I am not overtired." She bit her lips and tried staring at the carpet.

But, oh, he had also removed his shoes and the sight of his beautifully made bare feet made the heat burn brighter until she wanted to fling off the covers. Already the area between her breasts grew damp as she began to sweat.

"What is it you read?" he asked, stepping closer yet again. "What does an enterprising woman of business peruse at night, in her bed?"

Two more steps and he was at the edge of her bed. Honora jolted before she could stop herself, sending her book tumbling off her lap onto the carpet. He was like the approaching sun, emitting heat.

He reached down to pick it up. "*Gentleman Jack.*" He ran his finger down the book's spine and arched a brow at her. "Interesting. Nowhere near as enumerative as I would have imagined."

Honora swallowed.

"Are you fond of these sensational novels?" He looked right into her eyes, a searing, penetrating glance that would seem to Honora, did she not know better, amatory in its intention.

He had come to her bed before. They had...been together in the corridor at Ashland. But he couldn't want that now. It had been so long.

He dropped the book back onto the floor and sat on the edge of her bed. When he raised his eyes to hers again, Honora licked her lips, her mouth immeasurably dry. Somewhere deep within her body a drum began to beat, softly, but insistently.

"I thought, perhaps..." He put a hand on her leg, and though the blankets separated his touch from her, her skin burned on the spot.

Her leg jerked of its own accord. The left corner of his mouth lifted in a slow grin, confirming that with that one gesture she had betrayed his effect on her. A part of her wanted to wipe the smug smile off his face, but another, larger part sparked to the blazing look in his eye. She was hot, so hot, but stupidly gathered the blankets to herself.

He put his hand back on her leg, his fingers teasing out the shape of her knee beneath the blankets, and then higher, moving over the contour of her thigh. Honora's heartbeat responded in kind, escalating faithlessly. And when he began to gently tug at the covers, her breath caught in her chest.

He pulled the blankets off slowly, inch by inch, keeping his eyes on hers as he did so, the crooked grin lingering.

The covers came off and they both looked down at her legs, bared under the twisted nightgown. Once again he lowered his hand onto her leg, only this time it was his skin against hers, hot and solid and real.

Honora's eyes flew to his, certain of his intentions now but no less clear as to his motivation.

"What?" One shake of his head stopped her whispered imploration. That, and the way he looked at her, with a hunger and intensity she'd certainly never witnessed before, something like desire.

His fingers sought the edge of her nightgown and slowly, so very slowly, pushed it up as he skimmed the flesh of her leg. Up, up to the top of her thigh, and higher and...

Oh. Honora made a sound, an embarrassing squeak on an intake of breath as flames shot from his hand and directly into her blood. She felt flushed and wanton and desirable. His fingers went between her thighs, the white nightgown rucked scandalously up to her waist and his eyes bore into hers with curiosity and intention and... *Oh.*

She'd been reading; the room was brightly lit, illuminating every motion and every look. Her breath came fast, puffing from her chest in panting gasps as her eyes flew from his to his hand, his fingers doing something that made her toes curl. She was still coherent enough to feel a sense of shock as she watched her legs flop open, as she watched her body silently beg for more.

He answered in kind, pressing the heel of his hand against her as he rose up over her to pull down the neckline of her nightgown. Then his mouth lowered over her bared breast, fastening over her nipple in a hot, wet kiss that sent her arching against the bed. He held her like that, between her legs and her breast, as Honora's vision swirled, riding the edge of a painful, blissful knife edge. She knew what was coming, but this was nothing like the brief explorations she'd made of her body, his touch on her nothing like her own.

She arched and called out as it took her, a spiraling, blistering pleasure that did something to her bones, something that turned them to melted wax and immobilized her.

Ash watched it all, the corner of his mouth curving at this moment only for her. Before she could catch her breath, he lifted the nightgown off of her, slowly tossed it aside and then stood to remove his own shirt. Honora had yet to recover her vision, and watched him through a haze of receding bliss, unbuttoning his trousers and tugging them off. He turned to her, and she saw for herself the evidence of his desire.

He was absolutely beautiful, long and lean and entirely male. The sinewy curves of his perfect muscles glowed in the lamplight. Dark hair covered his chest and went downward, thickening between his legs.

He watched her watching him, and took himself in hand, moving his fist over the erection that sprang straight out from his body. "This is what you've done to me," he said in an unfamiliar gravelly voice that thrilled Honora to her core.

He came back to the bed, where she still sprawled like a wanton. Grasping her hips, he pulled her down so that she lay beneath him, and with little fanfare, thrust himself inside her.

It felt good; he filled her with a unique heat, but experience had taught Honora this is where things would change. She waited for the moment of disillusionment as he began to move, for him to quicken his pace and be done. Only, he held himself steady and when he moved against her it was slowly, deeply, and he did not appear to be in any hurry at all. His skin rubbed against hers, soft and coarse, the scent of him engulfed her. His fingers twined in her hair. The result was marvelous, sending a brand new tension spiraling through her.

Bringing her arms around his back, she took a chance and arched against him. He groaned, so she did it again. When he looked down at their joining, desire and mortification coursed through Honora. She must have made a sound, for his gaze moved back to hers.

"Do not be embarrassed. This is what our bodies were made for," he said hoarsely. He brought his thumb to her mouth, caressing her lips until they parted and his finger was gliding against her wet tongue. Then he took that thumb and rubbed it against her nipple, making her moan in a most indecent way.

Oh, yes, Honora thought. This is what she'd wanted, only so much better for she never could have fully envisioned the sensation of him atop her, inside her, surrounding her with his entire body. His body, both smooth and strong; his breath hot against her ear; the smell of him a part of her, around her and inside her. Never could she have imagined the sense of abandon that would overtake her at being so fully in his power, the blissful jolt as she arched against him and the pleasure took her again, and his answering cries sounded in her ear as he shuddered against her.

CHAPTER ELEVEN

"Gentlemen." Honora, from her customary seat at the head of the table, called the group to attention. One by one the men settled at their places at the gleaming table, leafing through the portfolios laid out before them. There were familiar faces, and a few new ones at this meeting of potential investors.

To her right, in his customary place, sat her secretary, Mr. Davies. "A secretary!" Ash had exclaimed when she'd mentioned him. "Then why in the devil are you working every minute of the day if you've got someone to do it for you?"

Honora had laughed in response, understanding his question as both teasing and earnestly serious, and earned herself a wicked grin. "Though Mr.

Davies is worth his weight in gold, it does not absolve me of my share of responsibility."

It had been a morning of surprises for his lordship. In addition to the existence of a secretary, Ash had been equally amazed to learn of the existence of the offices Honora kept near the waterfront.

"Offices?" he'd mocked, staring up at the giant building.

"It is one of our larger buildings," she'd allowed, following his gaze up the behemoth of brick and glass.

"One of?"

Honora shrugged. "Botham Enterprises is a many-faceted concern. Most of this building is for our use, the rest is rented out."

"My lady landlord," he said, grinning.

She stole a look at Ash now, in the chair at her left. Though the biggest surprise perhaps thus far for him had been finding himself included in this morning's meeting, he bore no sign of it. He lounged in his chair with careless grace, dreadfully handsome, nodding and smiling at the men speaking to him. She'd not mentioned to him that his presence hadn't been her doing; rather, he was here at the specific request of several of the potential investors. Honora cast a cool glance at each of the men in turn, certain they possessed motivations above and beyond currying the earl's favor.

It was, in truth, an odd feeling having Ashland there, like two distinctly separate worlds had suddenly collided. Which, she supposed, they had. There was the old familiar world of work and Botham Enterprises and reassuring panicked investors, and the new exhilarating world that Ashland had awoken, of flesh and desire, hours and hours in their bed. What would these men think, she wondered, to know that only hours before the earl's naked body had been entwined with hers.

She feigned interest in the papers before her, hiding the blush that stung her cheeks. Oh, the things they had done. She could hardly credit it.

Familiarity with his body did nothing to curtail her fascination with it. Night after night he came to her bed, and night after night she gasped and sighed as though it were the first time. He stepped through the door connecting their rooms, and her heart would begin to pound, sending her blood singing in an incendiary surge. He would stop and strip before her, watching her as he did so. Every time she enjoyed the titillation of it, greedily drinking in the sight of his bare skin. He was truly finely made, and there was no part of him she did not find beautiful. He was fit and lean and strong, and having him in her bed fulfilled all the secret things she'd so longed for from a man's body.

He took as much pleasure as he gave, with no small amount of effort. He seemed amply satisfied with her, a notion that, if she were the sort, could have made her swoon.

Her fear of incompatibility had diminished with their newfound sensual intimacy, the growing regret over her marriage had been replaced with the conjugal passion she'd dreamt of. But it was so much more. He was so much more. It was as if their sudden physical satisfaction with one another had unleashed something between them outside of the bedroom as well, a rapport fed by the current generated by their bodies.

Mr. Davies coughed discreetly, jerking Honora's attention back to the meeting.

Mr. Pearson, one of the new investors, who had evidently taken it upon himself to begin the meeting, appeared to be questioning Ashland on construction timetables.

"The dates are referenced in the documents that you were provided, sir," Mr. Davies said.

Mr. Pearson cast the poor secretary a dismissive glance and turned back to Ashland. "My lord?"

"As Mr. Davies said," Honora interrupted, catching Ashland's bemused glance as she pulled the aforementioned document from the portfolio before her, "the dates are all provided. Was there a question on a specific stage of the project?"

Pearson kept his eyes on Ashland. Mr. Davies scribbled on his notepad, noting, she knew, all the details of the current goings on. "What guarantee am I to have that the materials will be delivered before winter sets in?" A sense of misgiving flared in Honora's belly. Several of the other men shifted in their seats. Mr. Pearson was a new investor, one of the crop of newly rich men whom she was cultivating to subsidize her newest railway project.

But this was not Honora's first time dealing with panicky investors or overreaching men.

"Mr. Pearson."

Honora waited until the man finally turned his gaze from Ashland to her. She paused long enough that Mr. Davies put down his pen. "Perhaps you have had previous bad experiences, but I assure you that I do not go back on my word. Our timetable, barring an act of God, is firm. That being said, as any man of business knows, there are always unforeseen risks to any venture. You have the figures. Frankly, I believe this is a wonderful opportunity, but if you feel otherwise, or have doubts you cannot overcome, then you are free to go."

A heavy silence hung over the room. Honora knew her tone had been harsh, but this situation needed to be nipped in the bud as quickly as possible. Mr. Pearson seemed the type to relish control, and he needed to know he did not have it here. She did, and she would not allow him to sow discontent.

Pearson frowned at her, clearly unhappy at being told off by a mere woman. "Now see here, I've a right to have my concerns addressed. How am I to know you won't simply take my money and run this thing into the ground?"

Honora stiffened. "Indeed. And I will clarify any legitimate questions. I will not, however, tolerate a smear on my name."

Pearson scoffed and glanced at Ash. "Isn't it Ashland now? New ownership?"

Ashland did not answer, only watched the man with a scowl. The other men remained silent, those familiar with her knew that she would not be crossed, the other new investors biding their time to see which way the situation would evolve.

Honora rested her folded hands on the shiny mahogany table and exhaled audibly. She allowed a look of passing regret to cross her features. Mr. Davies took up his pen, aware that this was her favorite negotiating tactic: a preemptive, reluctant farewell. She'd learned long ago that taking something away from a man made him want it all the more. Granny had been particularly skilled at this approach, ending with making the man feel everything had been his idea all along. Honora, on the other hand, demanded that anyone working with her knew who was in command.

It was a game, after all, and she would win or walk away.

"I am afraid, Mr. Pearson, that this might not be the best venture for you. Perhaps—"

"Not at all," he interrupted, and then after a slight pause, "My lady. I didn't say I wanted out. Just need a bit of explanation before I put such a large sum in. You are perhaps being overly emotional about the matter. These types of things are discussed at length, in a man's world. You might not understand."

"No."

It was Ash's turn to deliver a surprise. Every head in the room turned to look at him. He leveled a narrow-eyed gaze at Pearson. "Lady Ashland is not being overly emotional. She is being more patient than you've a right to. You insult her position and her intelligence, and need I add, that an insult to my lady wife is an insult to me."

This naturally had the desired effect, and sent Mr. Pearson sputtering to recover ground. Honora bit her lip, fighting not to lose her so recently lauded patience. Ash continued to frown at Pearson, until the man had evidently apologized enough. With a curt nod, he ended the other man's misery.

The remainder of the meeting proceeded uneventfully, and by the end she was fairly certain that she would receive the investments she needed. One by one the men took their leave.

"I will see you shortly, Mr. Davies." Mr. Davies packed up his supplies and left the room, closing the door behind him. Honora turned to look at Ash, still seated in his chair.

"What an intolerable situation," he said before she could speak.

"What, pray, did you find so intolerable?" Something must have come through her voice, for his gaze sharpened.

"That man. And the way he spoke to you."

Honora made a small sound, and leaned her hip against the table. "I am abundantly familiar with men of Pearson's ilk. Do you really believe this is the first time I've encountered insolence or disrespect? I'd never do any business at all if I took offense."

Ash frowned. "Very well. You do not take offense, it is your prerogative. But not mine. No," he stood and approached her, "don't roll your eyes at me. You may abide by your own rules in this, but I abide by mine. That will never change. I won't ever tolerate anyone speaking to you in that manner."

Honora turned her gaze out the window, mainly to hide the surge of pleasure his words brought her. It curled deep within her chest and spread like honey through her limbs. She bit her lip, trying to quell it.

"Now," he approached her, "you are no doubt telling yourself that under no circumstances should you allow yourself to believe, or rely on my care. I realize," he rested his hands on the table, on either side of her hips, "how independent and bloody-minded you are, but..." He leaned forward until she looked up at him. His face inches from hers, she felt the warmth of his breath as he spoke.

Honora's heart began to beat heavily. Still, she forced herself to say, "You make me look weak. When you defend me. As if I cannot manage the situation."

He twisted her hips until she was facing forward, and stepped in between her open thighs. He rubbed one hand along her jaw, watching her intently. "Woe betide any man foolish enough to imagine that you are weak."

Then his mouth was on hers, hot and insistent, tasting of coffee and him. *Oh,* she wanted to say, *I am weak. You make me so.* Instead she gave herself over to his mouth, and his hands, and his hot delicious skin as he eventually rucked up her skirts and crinolines, unfastened his trousers and had his way with her right there, on the gleaming table of Botham Enterprises.

* * *

She was a secret fire, banked beneath an icy surface. She was lust and longing and things he'd never imagined. He'd seen her naked in the bath, spied upon her like a lovelorn youth, and ever since he'd wanted her with an intensity, unfamiliar and raw. He breathed in her skin, her breath, the secret musky scent between her legs. In bed, he licked her creamy skin, from tip to toe, and still he wanted more with a hunger that both fascinated and frightened him. He took her on the surface of the table, in broad daylight, wanting to possess and be possessed. Wanting to master her, but losing himself in her.

She was as hard to crack as a mystery, but when he did, when he felt the firm line of her mouth soften beneath his, when she welcomed his tongue with her sizzling heat, he was undone. She was like butter melting, and the more he had, the more he wanted.

She opened for him, answered his call by spreading her legs and taking him deep, her legs white pillars against the mahogany table. She flung her head back, panted in his ear, and he gave and took more, until they both shook with an intensity of release that had not yet failed to amaze him.

Afterwards, she pulled down her skirts and fussed at her hair while he buttoned his trousers. He reached out and adjusted her collar. She looked up at him with the liquid haze her eyes took on after sex, as though she had not yet returned to reality, a reflection of the tumult of his feelings.

It was only later, in the carriage that a question occurred to him. "If you did not want me to speak out on your behalf, why did you ask me to the meeting?"

She stared down at her glove for a moment and then glanced up, looking him in the eye. "The invitation was not mine. Your presence was requested by some of the gentleman. Pearson, most likely." Her dissatisfaction was evident in pursed lips.

Ash felt a stupid flare of hurt, realizing how very pleased he'd been at the thought that she'd wanted him there. He turned his gazed out the window, keeping his emotions off of his face. Still, she seemed to sense something was amiss.

"I never thought you'd care to be there."

"I understand," he said, with a flippant wave of the hand. "I have my uses, and the workings of the mighty Botham empire is not among them."

He'd the feeling she would say more, but she was quiet. And some ridiculous part of him wanted her to contradict him, to assure him that he was in some way, however miniscule, relevant to her.

* * *

When it was very late that night and Ash had not yet come to her room, Honora rose from the bed and went through the connecting door into his chamber. He was abed, she could see him in the moonlight that flooded through the windows, turned on his stomach with one arm flung over his head. He did not stir, yet she had the feeling he was not asleep.

"Are you upset because I neglected to invite you to the meeting?"

Silence. Honora waited and he eventually spoke. "No, I am not 'upset'. Chits in the schoolroom are 'upset'. I am merely tired." He turned over and peered at her through the darkness. The sheet shifted as he did so, and Honora could see his bare chest.

"I did not mean any offense."

"I am not offended."

"Then why—" she stopped.

"Why?" Ash waited. "Ah, why did I not come to your bed?" He folded his arms beneath his head and watched her.

She knew he wanted some sort of admission from her, something to appease whatever disruption to his emotions the meeting had caused. Honora debated returning to her room, and letting him stew, but such a gesture would deprive her as much as it would him. "Yes," she answered. "I did wonder why you did not come to my bed. And then I realized that you had a bed as well."

She stepped closer to the bed until she was certain he could see her very clearly. With one sure movement, she lifted her nightgown and tugged it off, dropping it onto the floor. Before he could speak or move, she climbed onto the bed and knelt beside him. "Although after a table, I suppose any surface is a possibility."

"*Honora*." He breathed out her name, and she knew he would not be asking her to leave.

She pulled back the sheet that covered him, exhilarated to find him naked beneath. Heart pounding like a maddened thing, she leaned over him and kissed him until his hands lifted to cup her breasts.

He sat up, kissing and caressing her, stoking the fire. Just when she was sure he would flip her onto her back, he shocked her by moving onto his knees. With firm hands at her waist, he tore his mouth from hers.

She'd imagined she had gained experience, that her body had become accustomed to the act of love. But when he moved behind her he dismantled her naïve notions, holding on to her waist, taking her, encompassing her, demanding more. At the end she cried out his name until it rang in the room and far beyond, until she felt his release and heard the hot whisper of his voice in her ear, calling her name in response.

CHAPTER TWELVE

T he Honourable Clive Wesley and Ash had been friends for many years, over which time they had caroused to the best of their limited fiscal ability; Wesley, as one of a handful of sons of an insolvent, countrified Viscount, was in even worse financial straits than Ash himself. Lack of money aside, they had always managed to search out the best amusements, drinking and wenching as befitted two aimless young aristocrats of limited obligation.

Wesley had been absent for some time, thus Ash eagerly received word of his friend's return to Town. Reading Wesley's scrawled note announcing his arrival, Ash was overcome with a desire for a bit of amusement, and there was no one as entertaining as Wesley.

It was ridiculous, really, his reaction to Honora's dismissal during the investor's meeting; it wasn't as if he didn't know what the devil was going on. But he'd had this obscure aspiration to be of some use, and she, in her perfunctory, blunt style, had made it abundantly clear that he wasn't. He was, he supposed, destined to continue living this shallow life as an accessory to his accomplished wife.

Not introspective by nature, such musings had left him out of joint, itching for diversion.

So when Honora stiffly informed him that afternoon that her courses had come and he would be unable to visit her bed, Ash clapped his hands together and smiled. "Perfect timing! I've just heard from Wesley and he's back in London, so I'll just see him tonight."

Honora's mouth dropped open and a bizarre collection of undecipherable expressions crossed her face in quick succession. She looked like she would speak but instead left the room without saying a word, her hands fisted at her sides. Ash began to comprehend just how taxing this time of month could be, and hoped it wouldn't always be like this. He decided to not interrupt her and left for the evening without bidding her farewell.

He remembered arriving at a semi-respectable party with Wesley, where a fine Scotch was consumed in great quantities. He vaguely recalled dancing girls, a hackney to a gaming hell, drink of far less quality, and Wesley urinating in an alley. He did not know if these events all took place in the same night, or whether they'd taken place at all. They were, however, the only thoughts flashing through the muck that was his mind the following morning when he woke, still clothed, on top of his bed. Bright sunlight edged around the curtains, sending spikes of pain through his head.

Ash groaned and turned over. Wesley was more himself than ever, still managing to make the night as wild as possible.

"Dammit it to hell, Ash. A married man. Does your wife want you home before midnight?" Wesley had cackled.

"Married I may be, but I am still master of myself," Ash answered dryly.

"So the leash is fairly loose," Wesley said with a sly look. "Or have you even tested it? Tell me, what have you been doing all this time?"

Ash had been eating well and staying home and happily bedding his wife, but he wouldn't tell Wesley that and risk more mockery. He'd only lifted a glass and drained it while issuing a challenging stare to Wesley, who picked up the challenge. That had been at the party, or possibly the gaming hell. Or maybe he'd imagined it.

He moved to sit up, groaning as he did so. His gut churned for a second, until Ash got the better of himself. It had been a good long while since he'd been in this state. He briefly wondered if it was worth it.

Of course it was, he chided himself! It was what they did, he and Wesley: They made merry. Their other companions, Cummings and Hornby, Ash had learned from Wesley, had the misfortune of being stuck in the country and unlikely to be in Town any time soon.

"Cummings' witch of a grandmother has cut him off without a penny," Wesley had told him. "And Hornby's father, as far as I know, plans on having him married off by the end of summer. He's gone to visit his beloved's estate in Scotland of all places."

Wesley looked positively ill at the nuptial misfortunes of his fellows.

It was thus incumbent upon the two of them to make merry for their missing fellows as well. Ash found himself out every night, and rarely home before dawn. He spent most of the day asleep and recovering from the night before, until he prepared himself to begin all over again. It was just like old times, if considerably more exhausting.

Only, there seemed to be a harder edge to Wesley, some undefined sense of animosity beneath his temper, a fleeting impression of rancor that Ash couldn't quite place his finger on.

Of course, Wesley was still penniless. Naturally Ash would pay their way, there was no question. But if he were honest with himself, there was something about the way Wesley simply expected Ash to pay for everything that irked him. They'd place their orders at the pubs and gaming hells, and Wesley would simply wander away, leaving Ash to cover the costs. It was the presumption of it, he supposed, and total lack of acknowledgement that was distasteful.

While Wesley wouldn't acknowledge that Ash paid for everything, he seemed to be obsessed with Honora's finances.

"How many houses does the countess own?" he asked, smirking.

"Your lady wife must never have to scruple in the household budget, eh, Ash?"

"Has she bought you any new horses?"

For the most part Ash shrugged off the comments, until Wesley would cross a line. Ash would push back, and Wesley would draw down. Until the next time.

If it weren't so laughable, he'd say Wesley was jealous.

After a while, Ash would have indeed preferred to stay in a night or two. Wesley was just as relentless in pursuit of amusement as he'd always been, and gaped at him when he voiced his opinion. "What, ho? Your lady reining in you in?" Wesley guffawed.

Ash frowned. In truth, he'd barely seen or spoken to Honora in over a week. She'd never expressed a wish for him to remain at home. It was a desire all his own. He found he missed their dinners and the quiet time in the drawing room afterwards, and he most certainly missed her in his bed. He was beginning to ache with it. However, he reluctantly let Wesley believe what he wanted, and said only, "A man has needs." Wesley could soothe himself by searching out a whore. Ash had a wife at home.

* * *

Honora, in her third excursion of the week with the dowager and Margaret, attended a dinner engagement. Socializing was Ashland's particular talent. In the times they'd been out together, she'd seen him navigate crowds with polish and ease, greeting old friends and effortlessly making new ones, like some sort of aristocratic snake charmer. He had the elusive skill of drawing people to him and the even more challenging ability to make Honora feel somewhat at ease in the company of his fellow aristocrats.

Honora's recent sociability stemmed not from a particular desire to mingle, but rather rose from the disinclination to sit at home like a forlorn fool, waiting on the husband who seemed to have lost the modicum of sense he'd recently gained.

Margaret seemed to take pleasure in her company, spending a good deal of time at her side, confirming Honora's earlier suspicion that the season and society were not as dazzling as the girl had pretended. Though it touched a soft spot in Honora's heart, she did wonder why Margaret, who belonged to this world, was having a difficult time, but sensed that broaching the topic would embarrass her. It wouldn't be a simple thing to admit that matters weren't progressing as well as they could in her debut year.

Lady Celeste, suffering no such difficulties, appeared to be enjoying herself immensely, patently making up for lost time. She had ceased demanding Ashland's company and seemed all too happy to attend balls and parties without him. Or perhaps, having somewhat re-established herself in the society she'd so missed, she considered herself chaperone enough for Margaret.

If Lady Celeste and Margaret wondered where Ashland was, they kept their questions to themselves. It was a testament to desperation that some part of Honora wished the dowager would mention Ash's ridiculous behavior of late so that she might at least in some way speak of it aloud. Lady Celeste, however, was so wrapped up in her own amusements that Honora wondered if she even noticed her son's absence.

There was no one to whom Honora might unburden herself.

Charlotte was too happily married, busy with the baby, living the life that Honora had so secretly yearned for. For a brief, silly moment she had thought she might have it. A semblance of a functioning marriage. Her husband in her bed, a baby in the nursery. She'd been near tears when her courses came, bereft with disappointment and then stung by Ash's casual dismissal. Surely he must realize how badly she wanted a child.

She supposed she could have borne it better had she not been so foolish as to harbor false hopes. She wouldn't even begin to consider what Granny would say.

In their hosts' drawing room after dinner, Honora spotted Margaret standing near a few girls her age. Perhaps it was Honora's imagination, but though the girl was talking and even laughing, there seemed something hollow in it, as if she were going through the motions. Honora privately cringed, taking in Margaret's gown, which was as usual, overdone just enough to stand out. She knew this was the dowager's doing. The woman seemed to feel that more was never enough: jewels, flounces, ribbons, lace, any embellishment that could be added to Margaret's attire generally was, as though making up for their years of deprivation. Lady Celeste's personal showy fashion preferences did not transfer so well to her daughter. Margaret had neither the bearing nor the age to carry off such ostentation and her clothing set her apart from the other girls. Honora suspected that Lady Celeste was browbeating her daughter, trying to recapture something that she missed from her own youth.

Embarrassing or not, Honora vowed to herself to speak to Margaret as soon as the opportunity arose. Indeed, she might need to mention something to Ashland as well, should he deign to grace her with his presence.

Soon they would return home. She did not expect to find Ashland there. She tipped her head down, hiding the frown she knew marked her features. She wouldn't admit it anyone, but oh, how she missed him in her bed. It had been so easy to become accustomed to the physical part of their relationship.

Taking a moment to hide her face away from curious eyes, Honora stood up and went to gaze at a painting, some gruesome outrage of a man on a horse surrounded by hounds and piles of dead foxes.

She was by nature reserved, and by nurture trained at concealing her emotions. And though a person could seldom read the thoughts on her face, it did not mean that she was devoid of feeling. In fact, she was all too full of feelings: wanting and needing and *longing*, for heaven's sake. The past few weeks with Ash had released something, and her emotions roiled forth, uncontainable and raw, and she really did not know how to collect herself.

Drawing herself up, she cast a glance at the people in the drawing room, and made her way to Margaret, Margaret who gave her a smile tinged with relief when she reached her side. Lady Celeste was engaged in a game of cards across the room, her merry laughter reaching them where they stood.

"Are you enjoying yourself?" Honora asked, watching her carefully.

"Of course," Margaret answered brightly, brushing aside the lace at her bodice. "And you?"

"I should be," Honora admitted. "It is certainly the expectation. One looks at the other guests, and they are obviously amused, yet I find myself mostly tolerating the situation until it is time to go home." Margaret frowned at the floor, until a glance across the room at her mother made her straighten up and smooth out her features into a vague smile.

"Do you ever find yourself, Margaret, feeling the same?"

"Oh, no. Not at all. Everything is so very diverting."

Honora would have said more, pressed the girl into her confidence, but could see she'd disconcerted her; Margaret's eyes shone bright and she fidgeted with her reticule. Honora patted her on the hand and let the matter rest, recognizing a fight for control when she saw one.

* * *

Much later, in the small hours of the night, sounds from her husband's chamber awakened her. There was a clattering and thumping, as though he'd fallen and in the process knocked a few things down. Honora frowned up at the canopy, a pervasive sense of frustration mounting within her. Frustration, it seemed, was to be the chief emotional response to her husband.

She sighed and turned over, determined to ignore him and sleep. For a while it was silent, then a renewed racket began, accompanied this time by muffled swearing. Honora rose from her bed and went to Ashland's door, pushing it open without bothering to knock.

A candle burned on the mantel, illuminating him and the room fairly well. He sat on the edge of the bed, one boot on, one off, stripped of his cravat and coat, his shirt partially unbuttoned. The room was in a fair bit of disarray; she'd been right about things being knocked over.

He looked up at her and squinted.

"It smells like a distillery in here, and an awful one at that."

He laughed, a wheezing sound that brought on a fit of coughing. "You are quite good," he rasped, "at conveying your disgust."

"Well." She looked at the candle. "I wish I needn't be."

"Naturally." He fell back on the bed with a groan. "I apologize for eliciting such revulsion."

Honora watched him silently for a moment, the rise and fall of his chest, one boot-clad foot swinging, as a sense of tenderness grew alongside her frustration.

"Aren't you tired of it?" she asked after a while.

She received no answer, and thought he must have fallen asleep. She turned to exit the room when he spoke, stopping her. "Of course I'm bloody tired of it. Do you believe this is the person I wanted to be?" He'd understood her question very well. "It's just this is the person I am, and I don't know how to change it."

This was far and above not the conversation Honora had been expecting, and she struggled with a response to his candid confession.

"I am born of wastrels," he continued. "I don't know how to be anyone else."

"Rubbish."

His head lifted from the bed to stare at her.

"You are not merely the product of your imprudent forebears. You are your own person, and, I believe, quite capable, should you choose to apply your efforts to an industrious cause. My grandmother—"

His head fell back onto the bed as he groaned.

"Yes, I mention her again. She rose from poverty by dint of sheer hard work and effort, and no little amount of intelligence. If she could do it, then you, with the benefits of your name and title can do just as well. Your fate is not prewritten."

"Damn me. Defended by my own wife."

The shock in his voice rendered her immobile. Was she truly so harsh with him, that he would be surprised to hear her speak well of him? She rubbed her forehead, unable to think, exhausted by how much effort marriage required. She wanted to go back to bed and *not* think about the charming wastrel that was her husband.

A soft exhalation came from the bed and she knew that he'd fallen asleep now. With a sigh she moved towards him, bending down to remove his remaining boot. Though not quite an easy task, her ministrations did nothing to disturb his intoxicated slumber. A snore issued from deep in his throat. The moonlight from the nearby window fell across him, etching the lines of his face in silver, as powerfully handsome in sleep as he ever was. Honora found a blanket and draped it over him, lingering to touch one of his outstretched hands, futilely wishing that things were easier between them.

"Sleep well," she said, and went back to her own bed.

* * *

Later, when she awoke to large hands on her skin and the warmth of Ash's breath against her neck, she kept her eyes shut, and let herself believe it was a dream. His breath trailed down her body as he moved over her, marking a path with his tongue, tasting and kissing. He rucked up her nightgown and nudged her thighs apart, his breath fanning the center of her, and still she did not open her eyes. When he placed his mouth upon her, she arched back, bit her lip, and kept her eyes tightly closed, existing only in this reality of his hands and mouth holding her hard to the bed, no thought of anything else but the pleasure he gave her.

* * *

"Wesley," he said, taking a seat in the study, "has a business proposition for you. It was initially presented to me," he said, brushing a speck from his trouser leg, "but I of course informed him that the business decisions were yours to make. My role being strictly ornamental."

She shot him a look distinctly lacking in amusement. She sat behind her expansive desk and he on the chair before it, an island of responsible mahogany between them. She was all business, gripping a binder as though she couldn't possibly put it down and give him her full attention. Disciplined and preoccupied, she frowned at him through the spectacles perched on the end of her nose. The feeling reminded him of being called to the carpet by his father, although Honora was far more sensible than his father had ever hoped to be.

To think that this brittle façade hid such molten depths. He thought of her beneath his mouth just last night, all heat and passion, and was amazed that this was the same woman. That ardor was now packed away and oh, how he wished he could access that secret nighttime Honora during daylight hours. Nighttime Honora was infinitely easier to communicate with, had fewer rules and reservations and was clearly more satisfied with him. He wouldn't mind replaying the events of last night. Right here, on her busy, busy desk.

His face must have betrayed some of his thoughts, for she blushed, and quite becomingly at that. "Pink is a good color on you."

Her mouth twisted, and though she tried to appear otherwise, he knew she was pleased.

"What is this proposition your friend has?"

Ash shrugged. "Something to do with shipping."

"I will hear him out, but I should tell you that I won't give favors simply because of your relationship. If it is not a sound venture, then I will decline involvement." She lifted her chin, daring him to disagree.

"As if I would ever imagine otherwise."

Ash glanced at the rain out the window. Truthfully, he was not particularly enthusiastic about Honora and Wesley meeting; they were from two different sides of his life, a before and an after, and he'd a silly, superstitious premonition that the parts shouldn't mix. But he could hardly refuse the request, though the occasion of Wesley making it had been so awkward he'd been tempted to.

"I've a brilliant idea to make us rich!" Wesley had exclaimed. "Make me rich, and you possibly richer," he amended in that new, sly tone Ash had come to heartily dislike. Then he'd gone on at length to talk about shipping and imports and cargo, meaningless things that Ash had let wash over him. When he had finally gotten a chance to speak, he'd had no choice but to explain that Honora, and not he, was the head of Botham Enterprises and that Wesley would need to take his request to her.

This had earned him a hard look, something dark momentarily twisting Wesley's mouth, a flash of disbelief, or scorn. Ash held his gaze until he looked away. He'd be damned if he were going to feel shame, or pretend to be master of money that his wife's family had earned. Of course, it had initially been a nasty shock to learn just how limited was his access to the money. But he'd known the scope of the work needed at Ashland, and he'd begun to have a taste of what it took to maintain Botham Enterprises and it hadn't taken long for him to realize that it was all better left in Honora's capable hands. He could admit to himself, if no one else, that he'd only muck it up.

"Don't worry yourself," he'd said tightly to Wesley. "The woman's a financial genius."

So it came about that Wesley was invited to dine. They would include William Sloane and his wife, and a few of his mother's guests. A proper dinner party.

* * *

They met in the drawing room before the other guests arrived. Honora wore a fluffy green confection that complimented her rather well. Wesley was clearly trying to ingratiate himself. He oozed an odd, affected charm when they met, one that Ash could see was having an off-putting effect on her. She was gracious in her role of hostess, but stiff. She poured the tea, made polite comments, smiled and nodded. She listened, tilting her head to the side, asking informed questions about the details of Wesley's plan, but to Ash she appeared far from delighted by Wesley or his proposition. He might not know everything about her or the business, but he did know enough to realize that a proposal during a meeting in the drawing room over tea was not one she was seriously considering. She was *humoring* him by speaking to Wesley. Why, she didn't even have one of her notebooks with her; she made no pretense of taking this seriously.

The indignation that jolted through him wasn't on Wesley's behalf. It was unlikely there was any merit to Wesley's scheme. It was the fact that she couldn't even bother with an honest effort, for Ash's sake.

She glanced at him, frowning infinitesimally at his stare. Wesley took no notice. He went on and on, peddling his scheme with obliviousness, his desire for riches blinding him to Honora's indifference.

Ash spoke out of the irrational sense of perversity he seemed to feel around his wife, fed no doubt by her casual dismissal of his intellect. "What a wonderful idea, Wesley. I'm sure it will be given the utmost consideration."

Honora blinked at him once and said nothing. Wesley smiled like a cat that gotten into the cream.

The Sloanes arrived and their conversation stopped. Ash ground his teeth in frustration and went and poured a drink for himself and the men. Sloane sipped carefully, while he and Wesley downed theirs and refilled the glasses quickly. He could see the look of deviltry in Wesley's eye, that mad glint that heralded uninhibited revelry. Some distant part of Ash's brain knew the wisest course was to turn away, to put down his glass and keep his composure. He quickly overrode it by pouring brandy down his throat.

* * *

Honora pasted a semblance of a smile onto her face, unable to summon anything authentic. She hoped no one would notice.

She was ridiculous. Petty and childish and just stupid. And so heartbreakingly envious that she thought she'd swoon from it.

She took a deep drink of her wine and signaled for more, watching the conversation around the table, avoiding Charlotte. Charlotte, her dearest friend, unable to suppress her joy, had before dinner shared the news in a secretive whisper that she was expecting another child. The news had struck Honora like a fist in the gut. She was not proud of her response, though she'd managed to express happiness. And she was happy for Charlotte, truly. It was only that she wanted the same happiness for herself, and it was very difficult to deal with the fact that Charlotte should be twice blessed in quick succession while Honora's chances of motherhood seemed to diminish every day. She was simultaneously happy for her friend and wretched for herself.

If wretched meant self-pitying and pathetic.

She looked over the rim of her glass at Ashland, laughing and chatting away as though he hadn't a care in the world. Which he hadn't. He'd no responsibilities, other than the indulgence of his own pleasure. He was never at home anymore, always out with Wesley, out and absent from her bed.

Yes, Ash. It was all his fault.

His partner in crime, Wesley, was making the most of his seat next to Margaret, paying her an undue amount of attention. There was a rosy cast to Margaret's cheeks that Honora had never before witnessed, and it was clear she was pleased by the attention. Mother Ashland, Honora thought derisively, appeared not to notice.

Sloane, seated beside her, spoke, and turned her attention away, bringing her out of her reverie. She was being a terrible hostess, she realized, drinking too much and ignoring her guests, and forcibly turned her thoughts to those seated near her. It worked for a short while, until somehow the topic of children came up. She noticed the exchange between Charlotte and Sloane, a quick glance of silent conspiracy, and the resulting smile tugging at the corner of Charlotte's mouth.

"Oh, how I simply long for grandchildren! Of course, times are so different. The priorities are no longer hearth and home." Lady Celeste, pronounced, with a smile at Ash, a downward flutter of the lashes that adequately conveyed her dismay at the childless state her son was subjected to.

Next to her, Sloane coughed quietly.

"Children!" Wesley nearly roared. "Gads, but I cannot picture you as the Pater, Ashland old man. You've too much the delinquent son about you." His face was red and shiny, and he'd clearly had too much to drink. But then, so had Honora. It beat within her chest like a warm fire, reddened her face and made her tongue careless.

"I wouldn't worry about it any time soon, Wesley old man," she spat out. "Ash is more likely to have children with you than he is with me, you spend so much time together." Honora tipped back her glass and drained it in one go.

Her comment was met with silence, the heavy and awkward kind that everyone loathed. It rested upon them for a long moment until it was broken by a loud bark of laughter from Wesley. He raised his glass in her direction. "How surprisingly coarse of you, my lady."

Charlotte, at that moment, spilled a large amount of liquid over gown, and needed to excuse herself, begging Honora to join her.

With a sigh, she left the table and led Charlotte out, summoning a maid as she did so. As soon as the door closed behind them, Charlotte whirled and stared at her, stunned. "Honora! Whatever has gotten a hold of you?" She clasped her hands to her chin, and Honora saw that her friend was genuinely distressed.

What could she say? How could she confess the depth of her envy to her dearest friend without sounding like the worst sort of person? She simply could not reveal all of it. So she settled on a partial explanation.

"I find Wesley rather aggravating, and my husband perhaps overly fond of his company. And," she looked away, avoiding Charlotte's concerned gaze. "It can't be a surprise to you how I long for children of my own. You know I am thirty."

"But I have never seen you act so... imprudent."

"You have never seen me working." Charlotte did not answer Honora's tentative smile. Honora continued, deciding on frankness, "Not all marriages are like yours, my dear. Our alliance was a matter of convenience, and we've the resulting relationship."

Just then the maid came to the door to attend to Charlotte's dress, and Honora breathed a sigh of relief. She could just make out the tightness of Charlotte's expression, her entire face shuttered against the unwelcome events of the evening.

Perhaps Honora had been crude, but she could not seem to care. Not that she'd ever wish to hurt Charlotte, but should she not have freedom in her own home to speak her mind? That damn Wesley got under her skin, and well he knew it. She hadn't missed the knowing smirks he'd alternately been sending between her and Ash. He could go hang. She exhaled loudly, her rage renewed.

"Honora." Charlotte dismissed the maid and Honora longed to follow her out. "Are you unhappy?"

The genuine concern on her face nearly sent Honora to her knees. Charlotte couldn't conceive of it, that she did not share in her happiness. Honora moved to her and took her hands. "Charlotte, dear. I wish I could say what you want to hear, but my situation is my own and while I am exceedingly glad for your happiness, you cannot expect others to have the same sort of marriage. It's rather unfair in a way, for naturally anyone would wish your experience for themselves." She smiled to soften her words, and Charlotte smiled uncertainly back, but the shrewd light lingered in her eye. Honora looked away from her gaze, focusing on her eyebrow lest Charlotte's distress undo her.

The wine had only served to exacerbate her already unsteady emotions, making her woozy and overly sensitive. She took a deep, restorative breath, making an inadequate effort to get a hold of herself. The control Honora prided herself on seemed to be ever dissolving.

They rejoined the party. Everyone had the good grace to pretend nothing untoward had happened, though Honora was certain as soon as the opportunity dawned she'd get an earful from Lady Celeste on her lack of decorum and inability to uphold the refinement due the Ashland name.

CHAPTER THIRTEEN

"You continue to be a surprising creature."

"Oh!" Honora jumped, hand flying to her throat. Ash was lying on her bed in the dark.

"Just when I think I've come to figure you out a bit," his disembodied voice continued from the dark recesses of her bed, "you do something so completely unexpected that it only serves to remind me that I don't know you at all."

Honora sat down near the window, in a puddle of moonlight. "Did I ruin your dinner party?"

"Oh, not all! It was infinitely amusing. Puzzling, I admit, but not ruined in the least. I don't think I've ever seen quite that shade of purple on Mother's face."

"Well, I shan't be apologizing to her," Honora said, lifting her chin. "I'll speak as I wish in my own home." This was to be her new dictum, she silently vowed.

"You may put down your shield. I never suggested otherwise. And I am aware that Wesley can be somewhat boorish."

"Somewhat?" Honora laughed. "I'd hate to see him at his worst." He made no move off the bed and she none from her chair, sinking into the intimacy of speaking in the dark.

"He's alright. Only incapable of taking things seriously. What news did your friend, Lady Sloane, give you? You did not seem yourself after she spoke to you before dinner."

Honora was glad the lack of light blocked the emotion from her face, for she was honestly startled that he'd observed that much about her.

"She gave me her happy news."

It sounded foolish, so foolish, and revealed a layer of pettiness and jealousy that Honora would rather keep buried. At the same time, it felt good to speak of it openly.

"Ah."

A single syllable that somehow managed to convey an unforeseen depth of understanding. Honora supposed her outburst had given much away.

After a minute, Ash spoke again, his tone too cautious. "I was unaware of your desire for children."

"Unaware? How could you possibly be unaware? Begetting an heir being one of the chief reasons we married."

"Well, yes, but I suppose I assumed it would be at some point in the future. I am only five and twenty."

Honora huffed. "Don't you know how old I am?"

His silence told her he did not. She made a sound too brittle to be called a laugh. "You really did not learn a thing about me."

"I'm learning it now," he said gently.

Honora sighed. From outside came the songs of the crickets and frogs, faint city sounds from the distance. Exhaustion hit her at once; she never imagined that marriage could be so physically draining. "I was thirty my last birthday."

"Thirty," he breathed, as though the number were incomprehensible.

Honora rolled her eyes. "I am not decrepit yet. But a woman must, at a certain age, begin to…" She found herself unable to discuss the topic with him in detail, to her very great mortification. "There is only so much time. And I have always wanted children." Wanted, longed for, yearned for, burned for.

"Damn me. An older woman."

Honora laughed. "I thought it was one of the reasons that you disliked me. I should have realized you'd no idea."

Ash didn't answer. The silence stretched and Honora supposed he'd fallen asleep. It was dark, after all, and late, and he was comfortably stretched out upon the bed. He startled her when he spoke.

"I do not dislike you. Whatever gave you such an idea?" He sounded so serious, but no, it must just be her imagination.

"Oh, I should say the curt language, physical distance, complete disinterest in anything about me or my work," Honora said. She reached down to slip off her shoes. She was so tired and longed for bed.

"I have been adjusting to a marriage I did not particularly want. It doesn't mean I don't like *you*." She heard him shift on the bed. "I like you just fine, as a matter of fact."

It was Honora's turn to be silent as she absorbed his words. It was all there, in his behavior, his actions... And yet, she supposed they did share a sort of fellowship, as different as they were. "Well."

"Have I surprised you so deeply?"

She wished she could see his face and better gauge the sincerity of his speech, for there was something indecipherable in his voice. She dropped her shoes and moved to pull the pins from her hair, tossing them on the vanity. "Indeed," she answered, really too exhausted to do anything other than take him at his word. "Thank you for speaking so openly."

Ash laughed again, a harsh chuckle full of dark amusement. "We at least have honesty between us. I don't believe either of us has ever felt the need to prevaricate. I'd say, in my humble, ignorant way, that we've a better foundation than most of our acquaintance."

A better foundation! With a shock she realized it was true, even as the denial formed on her lips. They always spoke honestly, a rather refreshing advantage she'd not considered. Warmth flooded her at the notion.

"So you have no issue with my age?"

"As I've only just learned about it, no, but I might be of a different mind tomorrow."

Honora stood and moved to ring for the maid. Suddenly Ash was up, stopping her with a touch at the waist.

"Do not ring for the maid," he said, his voice gone husky. His hand reached around her and pulled her to him, his breath fanning her neck. "I will assist you." He trailed his tongue over her neck and it was like fire shot through her blood, pooling in a delightful ache between her legs. She sighed against him, and let him remove the gown and everything else, and joined him in the bed, praying that the wickedness of their actions would not hinder the conception of a child, for surely such pleasure and shamelessness could not be rewarded. But under his body, under his touch and the heat of his mouth, she could not seem to care.

* * *

She pressed against him in the dark, her head on his chest, body entwined with his, wrapped in the alluring cloud of their shared scent. He traced his hand against her back, the curve of her spine a lullaby. She truly was a surprising creature. Starting with everything she said tonight and ending with her passionate response to him in bed, or against it as one position required.

An uncomfortable pit had welled up in his gut to hear that she thought he disliked her. What kind of man was he that his own wife should make such an admission so blithely, as though it were a fact she'd long ago accepted and expected nothing more?

Yes, he'd disliked her at first, more as a matter of principle, resentful at having had to marry at all.

But as he'd come to know her, he'd grown fond of her responsible, self-assured nature. She was outspoken and he never had to wonder if she meant what she said or was saying everything she meant; she clearly did. She was dedicated to his family and worked towards its regeneration, all while maintaining scores of business dealings, the intricacies of which he'd no idea.

If he were honest, his feelings were far more complicated than mere fondness. He did not know what to call the tangled mix of desire, need and reluctant hunger that now existed inside him. With her, he was a being both strong and powerless, in thrall to the sensations of her body and the passionate creature she became in their bed.

She slumped against him, asleep, her breath fanning softly across his bare chest. He lowered his hand to caress her backside, softly, as though in reassurance, not wanting to disturb her slumber.

And, children. Dear Lord, children. If he ever thought of them it was as some distant chore to tackle many years down the road. How terrifying. What kind of father could an irresponsible reprobate such as he be?

He knew what he wouldn't be: a deceitful charlatan like his own father. He'd be a better man simply by never harboring a secret second family, which he supposed was not a bad start.

He shifted a bit, keeping Honora tight against him. A child might be nice, he mused, ensuring the line and all that. He supposed she would want at least two, or more if they had girls.

He bit down the panic tickling his chest, telling himself to slow down. He'd already conjured a brood of children and himself as the beleaguered figure desperately trying to rein them all in. One child, to start. He could give her that. In fact, he'd heartily enjoy the practice.

He turned to her, moving over her as he gently settled between her legs. She sighed, a sound of half sleep and sweet acquiescence, and he entered her slowly, matching his breaths with hers as she clenched against him.

"A child. I can give you a child," he whispered into her hair, moving into her and with her, into oblivion.

* * *

Honora had attempted to arrange a shopping excursion with Margaret, a chance to attire the girl in something other than the busy dresses her mother preferred. Alas, Lady Celeste was not to be deterred and insisted up accompanying them, and what Honora had hoped would be a brief morning's distraction turned into an all-day affair. Lady Celeste would insist upon *this* milliner, and *this* perfumer, and *this* jeweler… She was very strong in her fashionable opinions. Honora did manage to exert some influence at the dressmakers, quietly telling the modiste to simplify Lady Celeste's appeals for more. Margaret was perhaps tired of looking like an over-decorated cake. Honora was certainly tired of seeing it.

She'd also been hoping for a chance to talk to the younger girl, and perhaps get to know her better. For all that they lived in the same house, they had hardly formed any sort of real acquaintance. She had only a brief opportunity for a short conversation while Lady Celeste chatted with a fellow matron.

"Margaret," Honora began, deciding there was not time for indirectness. "You should feel free to express your own wishes. In the matter of clothing or anything else. Certainly your mother is guiding you through the season, but I would always welcome your honest opinion."

The girl smiled somewhat ironically. "And how did your mother receive your honest opinions, Honora?"

Honora paused. "Well, I did not have the privilege of her opinion, for she died when I was very young. But," she quickly added, seeing the mortification on Margaret's face, "my grandmother, who raised me, always encouraged me to voice my thoughts. She may not have agreed with me much of the time, but she always listened."

"I'm sure you've observed enough to know that my own mother functions in a very different manner." They smiled at one another. "She means well, I know. It is my duty to accept her guidance."

"You are a very dutiful daughter, there is no denying." Honora was moved to squeeze Margaret's hand. "But you may also have some things, a gown for example, your own way, and you will be no less dutiful."

"There is not much I can do for my family, Honora, other than marry well. A marriage befitting the Ashland name. I know, I know, this is Mother's voice. But Ash has done his duty, and not merely by marrying your money. You truly are an asset to him, and to us." Margaret squeezed her hand in return. "I must do my share now." She shrugged and for the first time, Honora felt a deeper connection to her new sister, and was hopeful they could indeed one day establish a closer relationship.

"Perhaps I shall have some good fortune, and my duty shall not be disagreeable," Margaret concluded.

Honora let the matter lie, although she did not forget the conversation. Margaret, in her opinion, should have the freedom to marry as she wished. There was a tenderness to her that neither Ash nor Lady Celeste possessed.

Regrettably, the gentle conversation she started with Lady Celeste later that day in her study very quickly disintegrated. She'd thought to mention her concerns, to address the matter in a civil fashion, but Lady Celeste immediately took umbrage. In fact, she made clear, she had no use for any of Honora's opinions in regards to her daughter. Not on her wardrobe, nor on her spousal prospects. Their thus far peaceful cohabitation had been due to maintaining only the shallowest of interactions, and now that a topic of some honesty had been broached, the polite veneer abruptly cracked.

"I only mean to say that Margaret has the luxury of choice in her marriage," Honora stated. "She is well dowered and she can stay in our home as long as she cares to. There is no reason for her to hurry."

"No reason! Why, you cannot understand. I was engaged in my eighteenth year. Here is Margaret, having missed that opportunity, late to debut. What will they say if she is not engaged this year? Or the next? Pah!" Lady Celeste waved her hand, brusquely dismissing Honora's foolish notions.

"With all due respect, why should it matter what anyone says? Or if she is engaged this year or the next, or the one after, if it is her desire? She has a concept of familial responsibility—"

"I should think so! Though our circumstances were diminished our standards were not, and I hope that I have raised her well-enough that she knows her duty. You cannot understand," she repeated, a refrain Honora was more than tired of.

"I think it is you who cannot understand. Times are very different now." Honora rubbed at the spot between her eyes, which had begun to ache profusely.

"I understand well enough." Lady Celeste said in her iciest tones. "Times have indeed changed for you. And for your kind. In my day it would have been unheard of for a woman of your background to tie herself to an earl. We still maintain some of our standards, those we can. And I will decide what is best for my daughter."

With that she turned on one heel and left the room with a rather dramatic flourish. Honora could admire her finesse, if nothing else.

CHAPTER FOURTEEN

A sh had not expected Honora to finance Wesley's business venture. He was no businessman but even he had enough sense to know that spilling money into some poorly devised shipping scheme was an unsound investment.

'Unsound investment' was precisely the term Honora used when she broke the news to Wesley, having insisted upon Ash's presence when she did so. She was brief and not unkind about it, but he knew that Wesley wasn't happy to hear her refusal.

He kept the polite smile plastered to his face, but his eyes had gone decidedly cold, his manner brittle and sardonic. He made an attempt to convince her, pushing a stack of paper toward her, entreating her to look again at the numbers, the letter of guarantee.

"It very well might be that I come to regret my decision, Mr. Wesley, but I stand by it and shan't be persuaded otherwise. I encourage you to appeal to other investors, and you might find a different answer." She pushed the stack of papers gently across the desk back towards him.

Wesley regarded her for a moment, unmistakably debating whether to persist in attempting to change her mind. "I know a lost cause when I see one. How fortunate you are, Ashland old friend, to have such a strong-minded woman as your wife," he mocked. He stood abruptly and nodded, managing a smirk at Ash as he left the room.

Honora exhaled as he left, tapping her fingers against the desk. "He doesn't like my refusal," she said, staring at the door through which he'd passed.

"I should say not. But then who would?" He kept his tone light, but he hadn't at all liked the look in Wesley's eye

"This seems different. He's very resentful, can't you see it?"

"He'll settle down eventually," Ash assured her. "He'll find the money elsewhere and his vanity will be soothed."

Honora did not look convinced but let the matter drop, and they went down to tea.

Mother sat herself in the corner, keeping Margaret at her side, going on at her in whispered asides as the poor girl cast glum glances around the room. Honora took up the newspaper, becoming absorbed in some sensationalized story about a Duke's son that had run off with an American woman of low repute. It was a dismal day, damp, dreary with a steady rain that brought no improvement to the stale air, and Ash fought the urge to pace.

Perhaps it was the weather, or the particular tension that coiled through a stuffy room, but Ash found himself consumed with a growing nervous energy. The exchange with Wesley had left an unpleasant taste in his mouth. No wonder, as the man's bitterness had been palpable. But there was something else there, something new, unnamed, something that made Ash mistrust Wesley's increasing slyness.

It was just then that Neville announced a caller, cutting off Ash's train of thought. "Mr. James Goodson."

The name meant nothing to him. Honora, however, paused at the announcement, head tilted, recognition flickering across her features. Slowly she looked at Mother and Margaret, and then to him, her eyes large, lips pale and he wondered what caused her alarm until their uninvited caller stepped into the room and it was all too abundantly clear.

The boy was awkward but determined, his undeveloped chin all but shaking as he peered at them from underneath a wet mop of hair. He stood tall, though gawky, all arms and legs. He bore a significant resemblance to his younger brother, and a noticeable one to his elder.

James Goodson, the son of his father, stared at them one by one, fists clenched at his sides, until he spotted Ash, whereupon his face reddened and he took a step forward.

"Easy there!" Ash said, palm out, rising from his chair. Anger rose from the boy like vapor, or perhaps it was merely his wet clothing, beginning to dry in the warm room.

"What is the meaning of this? Who is this boy?" Mother asked huffily from her chair. Margaret looked on, brows knit in confusion.

Young Mr. Goodson glanced their way and then back to Ash. "Won't you introduce me?" he mocked. He pushed back his wet hair and carelessly flung the resultant droplets onto the rug.

Ash shook his head, unable to clear the jumble of his thoughts, the need to get the boy out of the room colliding with a dizzying fury at his presumption in coming here. He couldn't seem to form any words.

"It's good enough for my mother, is it?" James Goodson asked, disgusted. "You striding into her house and accosting her? But not yours, naturally." His voice rose with every word in crackling affront.

Honora stood and stepped towards the door. "Lady Celeste, Margaret, why don't we leave and let Ashland talk to this young man—"

"No!" James croaked, his face going even redder. Honora glanced at Ash, her eyes wary, urging him to calm. If his countenance betrayed even a trace of the emotions that were currently surging through him, then he must look a fright.

Ash took a deep breath and forced himself to think. If he guessed correctly, James's embarrassment was compounding whatever rage had driven him here. The young man lifted his chin in a stubborn gesture all too familiar to Ash; he'd seen it on his father countless times.

Lady Celeste gasped. "Ashland. What is happening here?" She half-rose from her chair, her sewing falling from her lap onto the carpet. She turned a gaze of deep suspicion towards the boy, clearly having recognized something in him as well. Margaret, wide-eyed, reached out an unsteady hand to restrain her.

Ash could not formulate an answer. Honora bit her lip, looking as stricken as he felt. He knew he had to handle this situation with great care, without upsetting his mother or sister, and also without further enraging this strange young man who happened to be his brother.

"This is between us," he said to James, marginally succeeding at keeping his voice under control. "You and me. Let's handle it like men, in the other room—"

"Ashamed of your bastard brother? Is that it?"

Well, what could anyone say to that? A shocked silence met James's caustic outburst.

Ash's first instinct was to look at Margaret, poor Margaret, always overlooked by Father, always waiting her turn, given only the dregs of his affection. She stared at the boy stunned, ashen. "Bastard?" she breathed, and even James looked away from the devastation on her face.

Honora took a step closer to Ash. She placed a hand upon his arm and a moment of warmth passed through him until he realized she did it not to reassure him, but to hold him back. She thought he would strike this boy.

The warmth quickly evaporated, leaving in its place a throbbing disappointment that her opinion of him remained so very low.

Inhaling as deeply as he could, he redirected his thoughts and addressed young James, giving him the confrontation he'd come here for and finally making an effort at getting the situation under control. "Watch your tongue, whelp. These are ladies." He cursed inwardly, but there was nothing for it, he must go on. "Yes. It is true. I did pay a call on your mother." He looked at his own mother, her white face confirming what he'd suspected: she'd had no idea about his father's second family. "Mother. This is Father's son. He had a younger boy as well. And…" If he called Mrs. Goodson a mistress, James would strike him, but he couldn't very well refer to her as his father's wife.

"He kept the children and their mother in another house," Honora finished for him, her tone level.

Mother stared at her, aghast, as though the telling and not the actions were shocking. "How long have you known this?"

"I learned of their existence prior to our marriage. When I had the family investigated. I did not realize they were unknown to you until later." Honora glanced at Ash.

Margaret began to cry, a soft yet unmistakable sound. Young James flushed even darker, clearly discomfited by all the emotion in the room. He stared at Ash, jaw clenched, his attempted fierceness dulled by the fat drop of water that rolled down his nose. He trembled, either with the urge for a fight or from being soaking wet, or possibly a combination of both.

"Does your mother know you are here?" Honora asked the boy. She spoke in the tone of women everywhere addressing rude young boys, and suddenly the air in the room began to change, James's belligerence reduced to sullenness, and he became a naïve lad rather than an imminent threat. At any rate, the damage was done: the news of his parentage was out, and there was no going back.

James looked truculently at Honora. For a moment he seemed that he wouldn't answer, but then gave a curt shake of the head. "She thinks I'm at school."

"And what is it you hoped to achieve by coming here?" she asked.

James looked at her, clearly mortified. Whether she realized it or not, with that one question she belittled the entire spectacle of his appearance. It was clear to Ash, after all, that the boy had come for a fight, a confrontation with the man who'd upset his mother. He couldn't very well confront their father, the man who was actually responsible for the awkward situation they all found themselves in. He could blame Ash in Father's stead, and find a tangible target for his rage.

As though reading his mind, James dove at Ash with fists furled, and made a solid attempt at doing him some damage. But Ash was quicker on his feet and stronger, and easily deflected the attack. He quickly restrained James, wrapping his arms tightly around him, a parody of brotherly affection. James growled in impotent rage.

"What insolence!" Mother screeched. "You should be thrashed!"

"I am not a child!" James yelled, the crack of his voice painfully indicating otherwise. He bucked, making an effort to escape Ash's arms, but Ash would not release him. Not yet.

"I won't oblige you with a fight," he said, giving him a shake. "And I can understand why you've come here—I should have expected it. But you need to get a hold of yourself."

When he eventually nodded, Ash let him go. James pushed himself away, muttering, with nary a peek at any of them. He looked tired and rumpled and undone by the enormity of undertaking this challenge on his own.

Ash felt an unwelcome bit of pity move through him. He once again extended his palms, trying to maintain a semblance of control, using the calmest voice he possessed. "Why don't we sit down, and have some tea?"

Every head in the room turned to him, astounded. "Well, what else can we do at this point?" Ash genuinely did not know. And tea was always a good idea.

"We should send a message to his mother," Honora interjected.

"Absolutely not!" James cried.

"We will have a room for you tonight but she should know where you are," Honora replied impatiently.

"I'm not staying here!" James, disgusted, appeared as though he were about to dash out of the door.

"Well you certainly aren't going anywhere," Ash said firmly, pointing a finger at an empty chair until James seated himself, with great, showy reluctance.

"Margaret, you will see me to my room at once!" Mother commanded.

"No, Mother," Ash said. "You will stay as well. And Margaret. This is a family matter." Taken aback, she re-took her seat, shooting James the kind of contemptuous glare she typically reserved for Honora. Margaret reluctantly sat down beside her, hands clutched in her lap. Ash scrubbed a hand over his face. If he'd ever been in an odder situation, he could not recall it. He gave himself some time to focus as they waited for fresh tea, letting the awkward silence unfurl across the room.

What the devil was he supposed to do now? He couldn't thrash the boy, much as a part of him might want to, for another part of him understood him all too well, and even respected his courage in coming here to have it out. He couldn't send the boy home alone in the growing dark and he couldn't just send him on his way into the middle of London. But how could he keep him here, under the same roof as his mother? The woman could be a nuisance at times, but the news of his father's other family had certainly hit her very hard.

Honora concentrated on pouring the tea, slipping extra biscuits onto James' plate. The boy might be defiant, but he was also hungry, and ate everything she handed him straightaway.

What a muddle. He looked at the boy, who glanced at him with a frown and quickly looked away. But Ash was the earl. And the son, and the brother, and the man to whom the responsibility fell.

"You will stay here for the night."

"The hell I will!" James exclaimed, jumping from his seat. At the same moment Mother gasped.

"Mind your manners," Ash bit out. "I remind you again there are ladies present. Now ask their forgiveness and sit down."

James looked like he would pop. His face, improbably, got even redder, and Ash would not have been surprised to see steam coming from his ears at any moment. But he must have had at least some semblance of breeding, for he tersely apologized to the ladies but refused to sit back down. Ash sighed inwardly, wondering if this is what a parent might feel like.

"Ashland, that you should even consider keeping him under the same roof as myself and your sister is absurd!" Mother said. "You shall not insult us so."

"It's hardly an insult!" Honora exclaimed, shooting a dark look at Mother. "The boy has nowhere else to go. Would you see him turned out into the street?"

She would, no doubt about it.

Honora looked to Ash, her brows raised high in disbelief. "Surely you won't allow this!"

It wasn't a question. It was a command, given in her imperious, commanding voice that just at that moment worked like a burr under Ash's saddle.

"What do you take me for?" he barked. Even James' gaze snapped to him.

Honora's expression hardened, the lines and shapes of her face shifting into a mask of extreme aggravation. "I hardly know what this family is capable of. In my time with you I have learned only to expect the worst."

Ash took a step toward her so that he was close enough to speak into her ear. "This is not the time for an airing of my shortcomings. Should I need your advice, I will ask for it!" He looked down at her, taking in the fury shooting from her eyes.

Louder, he repeated to the room, "James will bide here for the night." James's exclamation of disapproval was matched by Mother's. "I regret if it offends you Mother, but we can't in good conscience send him on his way alone."

"You can't keep me here!" James shouted, eyes bloodshot with fury. He really was no more than a boy, though he might believe otherwise, still a long way from manhood. Ash recalled the feeling well, standing on the cusp between childhood and adulthood, and this boy had a lot more on his shoulders: he was, after all, the man of the house, and a bastard to boot. Still, Ash was now responsible for his safety.

"I will lock you in your room, so help me God!"

Honora threw up her hands and turned her back. Mother moaned and flung herself backwards into the chair. Margaret watched Ash with a particularly wounded expression that cut him to the quick.

After a bit more dialogue and persuasion, James was grudgingly escorted to a room and Ashland determined to take him home the following morning. Ashland instructed a footman to stay outside for the duration of the night. He was, at this point, fairly certain the boy would stay put, but decided not to take any unnecessary risks.

Mother took her leave as well, forcing Margaret away with her, without a word from either of them to Ash. He thought Margaret might cry, so injured did she appear, and gave her a tight smile as she left.

Ash immediately poured himself a restorative beverage, drank it down in one go, and poured another. "To an unanticipated turn of events," he mocked, raising a glass in salute. His wife found no humor in it.

"You'll have the devil of a time on the journey tomorrow if you overindulge in drink now."

Ash swallowed the brandy, savoring the heat that was already spreading through his chest. He shrugged. "You underestimate me."

Her mouth twisted. "Do not judge the child by the father's sins. You mustn't unleash your anger upon the boy."

Ash stared at her and she stared back, flint-eyed. "After believing me capable of evicting them from their home, I thought you couldn't have a lower opinion of me. I stand corrected." The words couldn't completely mask the disappointment he felt again, foolishly, at that fact. Yet, was it ridiculous to want his own wife to have a decent opinion of him, to see him as something other than a callous ruffian? At the moment, it was too much to unravel. He took another drink.

"How long do you anticipate being gone?" she asked, unaware of the battle within him, or the effect her words had upon him. "I will need to notify Mr. Davies."

The change in subject had him puzzled. "Whatever for?"

"I must make arrangements if I am to be away for a lengthy period."

She assumed she would accompany him. Not, he ventured, because she intended to provide support or take her place at his side. She expected to go with him to oversee things and make certain he didn't bungle matters with his own damned brother. "You aren't coming." He spoke slowly, purposefully, as determined as he'd ever been about anything.

She stopped, stared at him. Tilted her head as though she were unsure of what exactly she were seeing. "What?"

"You. Are not coming with me. I will take him back myself. What is so funny?"

"That is not a good idea," she exhaled, a brow raised in what he clearly recognized as irate amusement.

"And yet, it exists."

Honora drew a deep breath, as though fortifying herself, folding her arms primly across her chest. "Ashland," she admonished. "You barely kept your composure on our visit to Mrs. Goodson."

"Thank you for reminding me."

"Frankly, this is a troubling issue for you, and I believe you would benefit from my company. And advice."

"My lady." He slammed his glass onto the table. "I find myself overcome with your advice. It is more than sufficient. He is my brother, I will deal with it," he bit out.

"And I am to stay here and console your mother?" she asked derisively.

"You know, I hardly care."

Her face went white, her chest rose on a deep inhalation.

"I suppose I'm able to make my own decisions," he continued in a tone much calmer than he felt. "Perhaps you think I'm too simple to notice, but I understand the attitude you have towards me. I daresay I'm not as clever as you are, but neither am I as foolish as you make me out to be. This is my family and I will see to it. Alone."

A wave of remorse flashed through him as she flinched in response. She quickly recovered her composure, however, staring him down with clear contempt. "Of course. How dare I assume I am any part of the illustrious Ashland family? I might finance all of you, take your sister in hand and see to the restoration of your much-mentioned former glory, but I am not a member of this family. Nor will I ever be. Thank you, for the kind reminder. I shall endeavor to never forget it again."

She turned and quit the room, leaving him with a dozen competing emotions: regret, righteousness, relief, shame and above all, confusion. He both wanted to call her back and wanted her gone. He was sorry for the turn things had taken, and yet he felt he'd reached a breaking point and could not, would not back down. What he'd said had been true: he was tired of being assumed an idiot.

Still another part of him longed for her advice, for there was no denying her fierce intelligence. Foolish, foolish man. He poured another glass and drank it down, fire and silk, not caring how he felt on the morrow.

* * *

Honora stared out the window at the departing carriage. He was really doing it, taking this upon his own shoulders, callously telling her to stay out of it. Ashland had only said he expected to be gone for a week. What his detailed plans were, he had not seen fit to share.

Margaret and the dowager apparently felt the same, neither sparing a word for her at breakfast this morning. Lady Celeste, who harbored no particular fondness for her, she could understand, but it had hurt to have Margaret rebuff her. When she'd managed to catch her alone in the hallway, all she would say was, "I'm astounded that you knew about this, Honora, and did not share it with me," and quickly hurried away. Somehow Honora came to be smack in the middle of this ugly situation.

Perhaps she might be a bit insistent at times. It was her nature, she supposed, making decisions and issuing instructions. Was she unyielding? Had she judged her husband too harshly? He'd been insulted when she cautioned him to show compassion to the boy. He expected her to have a better understanding of him. To trust him. And she'd bungled the situation entirely.

She never could have imagined, before, just how thorny married life could be, the endless difficulties between them, and dozens more coming their way. The Ashland life was so different from her own life with Granny, where the concerns of employees and staff had been far less emotionally complex than those she faced now, dealing with the legitimate and illegitimate branches of this one complicated family.

She saw now that it went even deeper. The old earl had been a blackguard, upsetting the lives of so many people to satisfy his own selfish whims. Honora may have had an unconventional upbringing, but she had been loved and valued. Ash and Margaret hadn't been afforded the same privilege, and she couldn't envision that the Goodson children had fared any better.

She gazed out of her study window at the pristine blue sky, heard the squawks of children playing nearby. Her hand moved absently to her abdomen, as though caressing the child that she hoped would one day rest there, wondering if motherhood, too, would be more complicated than she could imagine.

* * *

An urgent letter arrived from Mr. Davies later that week, explaining that there had been bad news in the railroad venture and requesting her immediate presence at the Botham offices. When she got to the building, her secretary wasted no time in updating her on the newly-arisen problem.

"It's Pearson, my lady. He's not only withdrawn his support, but convinced several of the other men to do so as well. Without them..." He trailed off, but she didn't have to hear his words to know the extent of the damage. Without the other investors, the deal was lost.

"This is awfully devious," she fumed.

"Indeed," Davies replied. "Seems to me as though they are working to steal the investment from under our noses."

"That is precisely what they're doing." Futilely, she wished she'd thrown Pearson out at that first meeting, when he'd been so openly disagreeable. Granny had always counseled against second chances.

Honora bit her lip. Ash, with his smooth, easygoing charm, would be an asset in negotiating with the withdrawing investors, and in reassuring those who might be having second thoughts. He might also serve in doing bodily harm to Pearson. How he would laugh at her now, after she had scolded him for intervening on her behalf with Pearson at the investor's meeting.

The tumult over the investment collapse caused Honora to cancel the outing she'd planned with a stony-faced Margaret, who placidly told Honora she was resigned to being overlooked and fled before

Honora could make amends. Later at home, Honora took a moment with Lady Celeste to voice her concerns about the impact matters were having on the girl.

"Margaret seems very low," she said, coming straight to the point.

Lady Celeste practically scoffed. "And is it any wonder, with the revelations of this past week? I cannot come to terms with it myself. That that *boy* should have the gall to come here and confront us." She pressed bony fingers to her lips. "And that you never mentioned a word to us! It beggars belief."

Honora bit down an angry retort, merely stating, "Ashland did not wish to disturb you with such news. Were it up to him, you would never have learned of Mrs. Goodson and the boys."

Lady Celeste flushed red, her eyes narrowing to half-slits. "Appalling."

Honora knew that she was commenting on Honora and not on Ash.

"It was not my secret to tell. If you've an issue with it, kindly take it up with your son. I daresay he is old enough to bear some responsibility in his life." And she promptly left the room, vowing to find the dowager separate lodgings as soon as time permitted.

* * *

Virtually all of Honora's time over the next few days was spent away from home, at the Botham offices, or knocking on the proverbial doors of the investors that Pearson had discouraged. In her meetings with these men, she learned the extent of Pearson's manipulations, how he had lied to discredit her and the Botham name. With little digging, she was able to confirm that Pearson was indeed stealing her investors with the goal of funding his own scheme.

She was disappointed in the perfidy of the men who'd known and worked with her and her grandmother. They knew her to be an upright woman of her word and previous investments with her had fattened their pockets. She wanted this project to proceed, and she needed these men to do so. Honora worked to arrange a meeting with her investors, personally convincing a few reluctant men of the benefits of hearing her out.

But for the first time she wondered if it was worth it. Botham Enterprises would lose money, yes, but not enough to do lasting damage. She thought the same might not be true for Pearson and some of the other men that had betrayed her.

Granny, she knew, would tell her to set aside her bruised feelings and move ahead. But, Honora thought, what had they worked so hard for if they must cater to the likes of these men? For if she got richer, so would they.

She wondered, but she would go forward; it was the only way she knew.

Such were the thoughts volleying through her mind as she arrived home late again, the house dark and quiet, as though it had already gone to sleep. Ashland was not yet returned from his journey, and she was not sure if Lady Celeste and Margaret had gone to their rooms or were out at an engagement. Their paths had barely crossed and Honora had postponed more than one excursion with Margaret. Overcome with a sudden craving for companionship, she thought she might even welcome a disparaging exchange with her mother-in-law at the moment.

She settled into her room with a supper tray and a large stack of files, with the intention of applying herself to a few more hours of work. Instead, she found herself picking at her food and ignoring the documents on her bureau, unable to quiet her thoughts or achieve the sense of tranquility she usually found in her bedchamber.

It was Ashland, she realized, that she really wanted.

She wanted to tell him about her outrageous notion to cut her losses and abandon this deal. She'd tell him that it went against everything that Granny had ever taught her of persistence and determination, and then listen to his remarks on the scope of Granny's advice and eternal guidance.

She missed him. She'd gotten used to his presence, his scent, his body next to hers. She'd come to enjoy his particular outlook on life, his irreverence a welcome balance to her own more serious nature. How she'd like to look over right now and see his crooked smile and that wayward glint in his eye.

She wanted to rest her head on his chest and listen to his rumble of laughter, to feel the reassuring solidity of his presence.

But he was so very far away, farther even than the miles that physically separated them and she did not know how to bridge the distance between them. Honora rubbed her eyes, tired, and alone.

* * *

She woke to a commotion. The pounding of feet running down the hallway, voices, a muffled shout. Honora sat up in confusion, pushing her hair out of her eyes, trying to see the clock from the chair where she'd fallen asleep. It was too early for whatever was happening.

Then the door flew open and Poppy rushed in, a hand clamped over her mouth.

"Poppy! What in the world is it?"

"Oh! My lady!" Poppy got out, her eyes large over her hand. Something sank in Honora's belly, a sickening plummet of unnamed panic that had her clutching her own mouth.

"Poppy. Is it Lord Ashland? Has something happened to him?"

Poppy shook her head, sending her little cap bouncing onto the floor. She stooped to pick it up. "Oh, no, my lady. It's Lady Margaret. She's gone and run off."

The confusion and relief that swarmed through her left Honora just as shaken as the panic. "Margaret? Where could Margaret have gone?" Surely Poppy was mistaken. Margaret was the last person to run off. Margaret was her mother's shadow, dutiful and quiet. She hadn't the pluck.

Poppy took a breath. "She's run off with that Mr. Wesley! She left a note."

"Wesley? Why?" Honora asked in disbelief. She could not begin to grasp why Margaret would run off with Wesley of all people, with whom, to Honora's knowledge, she had exchanged no more than a few words.

"They have eloped, my lady," Poppy breathed, aghast. "He has taken her and ruined her!"

Ruined seemed a rather harsh word, Honora thought dimly. She stared dumbly at Poppy and Poppy stared back at her until the urgency on the maid's face penetrated Honora's shock, waking the logical part of her brain. *Margaret has eloped with Wesley!*

And the household was waiting for Honora's guidance.

Honora made Poppy repeat the entire story, just to be sure, but it was no less true in the retelling. Finally, she shot to her feet and with a deep, calming breath, began issuing orders. Time was of the essence, but Honora knew the value of keeping her composure in a crisis. She sent a discreet servant to Wesley's dwelling for any information he could glean on his whereabouts, and asked Poppy to assemble the staff. With the household in an uproar, it was no longer possible to keep the matter contained. She did her best to stress the delicate nature of the circumstances, but could not worry about the servants gossiping: the priority was to get Margaret back as quickly as possible.

After a brief meeting with the staff, she was able to ascertain that the last anyone had seen of her had been last night at nine o'clock, therefore Margaret had most likely fled somewhere in the wee hours of the night. Her maid had found the note this morning in her unoccupied room.

It was a short missive, in content and tone.

Have gone to marry Wesley. M.

Really! As though the chit couldn't come up with better in the face of a scandalous elopement.

Honora tried to quell her spurts of fury in order to keep her mind focused, her thoughts churning over the best possible course of action as she hurried to prepare her departure. In Ashland's absence, she knew she must make haste and do her best to stop them before Wesley's plan somehow succeeded. She had suspected that Wesley had some under-handed plan afoot, although she never could have guessed it would be as devious as absconding with his friend's sister, nor could she imagine that this was the sort of treatment Ash desired for his only sister.

The servant finally returned from Wesley's home with news that the man had travelled north. North, to Yorkshire, where the servant had learned

Wesley had a family home. After all this, and hastily packing, and dashing off a letter to Mr. Davies to cancel the meeting with the investors, Honora made to depart.

Lady Celeste stopped her in the hallway, her eyes wild, her normally immaculate appearance in disarray. Hair trailed from her braid over her dressing gown, which she'd probably never before worn outside of her bedchamber. "Honora," she shrilled, "I should not have to inform you that this is a catastrophe!"

"I'm well aware, my lady," Honora replied, struggling not to snap at the woman.

"Margaret was overset with all this nonsense, with that boy! That terrible…" Honora knew she wouldn't say the word bastard, though she was clearly thinking it.

"We can hardly lay the blame for this at his feet!" Honora pushed her hands into her gloves, Lady Celeste's behavior only feeding her anxiety. "I've yet to hear you blame the one person who deserves it: your late husband. It was he who fathered those children!"

The dowager paled, and gasped with one white hand at her throat, as though Honora were physically attacking her. "Oh! You wretched girl! You know nothing about my late husband."

"I know enough, madam. Now, excuse me, I have more pressing concerns at the moment." Honora turned on her heel with a satisfactory swish of skirts, and sped through the open front door to the waiting carriage, and was away.

Honora managed to pen a quick note to Ashland, alerting him of the turn in events and of her plans of pursuit, hoping he would meet her on the road. She'd considered and discarded the idea of traveling by train; the last thing they needed was an uncontrollable delay. With so much uncertainty as to the outcome, the carriage would also afford them a measure of privacy once Margaret was found. In addition to the coachman, she had surrounded herself with several strong footmen and a few men from the stables, all of whom were armed. She would take no chances, Ashland or no. Though she sincerely hoped he would appear in time, otherwise she might have to shoot Wesley herself for his scheming temerity.

Once she was in the carriage and the hectic swirl of activity had stopped, a terrific headache born of fury and fatigue blossomed behind her eyes. She rubbed her head to little avail, and thought of all the ways she had disappointed Margaret. To be fair, they had all disappointed Margaret. The dowager, Ash, Honora. They had let her wane in the background, prioritizing everything ahead of a nineteen-year-old girl who had spent her life constrained in a dilapidated country house.

And wasn't that how life was, Honora thought, likely to change in an instant. She'd assumed she could give Margaret more attention at some future point, when other matters weren't as pressing, when she had the time... And Margaret had gone and taken matters into her own foolish hands. There was a lesson there, about waiting and the moment that she couldn't quite wrap her aching head around.

Fortunately, Ash appeared after a while, emerging on the horizon as a cloud of dust, only becoming clear as he reached the carriage. Dismounting from his panting horse, he slammed into the conveyance and they were instantly off again. He sat down unspeaking across from her, his face a mask of grim rage, obliterating any speculation she'd had as to his reaction to Wesley's treachery, and any fear that she'd overreacted in pursuing them.

Honora waited for him to speak, though his jaw seemed too tight to do so. Finally, he turned to her and brusquely asked what happened. Honora filled him in on the little she knew, omitting any editorializing on the base nature of his wastrel friend, which she imagined he knew well enough now.

"Damn!" He punched his own thigh, a mighty blow that made Honora wince. Somewhat tentatively, she moved to his side, and took that tight fist in her hand.

"We will find them."

"And what then? They'll be married and if not, she's already ruined. Damn his eyes." He pinched the bridge of his nose with his free hand.

"We'll shoot him either way," Honora said and Ash shot her a glance, judging her seriousness. She looked back at him. "Although, if I had to wager, I'd say he'll go quietly with the right price."

"He won't hurt Margaret," he said, although if he was reassuring himself or her, she didn't know. "He's greedy and stupid, not malicious."

Honora squeezed his hand. They rode in silence for a while, swaying with the rushing carriage. When it began to grow dark, and the horses and men could take no more, they stopped at an inn. Ash looked as though he would walk the rest of the way, pacing and tense as a caged animal, but Honora coaxed him inside, promising food and news from the innkeeper. They were lucky: Wesley and Margaret had indeed passed this way, and less than a day before. If the luck held, they should overtake them the next day.

As soon as Ash heard this information, he was out the door to the stables, calling for a horse.

"Ashland! Are you mad?" Honora picked up her skirts and raced after him. Coming to a halt in the open stable door, she found him arguing with the stable boy over a horse. But there were none to be had, their own animals exhausted, and only an old nag as a spare, which wouldn't get him to the next village.

"We will catch them up tomorrow. Come," she grasped his arm and steered him back into the inn. "Tomorrow. We all need our rest."

* * *

Ash let her lead him back into the inn, into the warm yellow light that waited there. He'd never felt so helplessly angry in his life, not even in altercations with his father, or even when encountering his father's second family. That Wesley had turned out to be such a scoundrel!

He saw it now, what the changes in Wesley's attitude had been: jealousy, all this time, of Ash's new wealth, and the opportunities it afforded. He knew Wesley had been displeased when Honora declined to invest in that stupid shipping venture, but he never could have imagined his oldest friend would take matters as far as absconding with his sister. It was an action born of greed, but not without malicious intent.

He followed Honora up to a room, ate the food placed before him, and drank down a glass of terrible wine. He laid down upon the bed, not bothering to get under the covers, and tried not to choke on his rage. Honora moved about the room, preparing herself for sleep.

"Did you have any inkling," she asked, focusing on the wash basin, "that Wesley could ever do something like this?"

"Of course not!" he bit out.

"Easy." She raised a hand in supplication. "I'm not accusing you, only trying to wrap my head around how matters got to this point." She sighed. "We have let Margaret down greatly."

"We?"

"Oh, yes." Honora sat down on a footstool near the fire. "For I have seen for some time that she was neglected and unhappy, and always some other matter pushed my concerns for her out of the way."

"Yet you wasted no time in racing after her." How tired she looked, worn-out after days or traveling.

"You are surprised." She sounded sad. "Despite what you may accuse me of, I am a part of this family. I care for Margaret. For all of you," she said, turning her gaze away.

Something moved through Ash, a shifting of notions and beliefs that felt like fire in his blood. "All of us? Even Mother," he joked, anything to gain a moment to cover the sudden tumult of his emotions.

"Some more than others," she answered wryly, and then lifted her gaze to his, as open as he'd ever seen her. It was like looking into a murky lake that had suddenly become crystal clear; he could see straight to the bottom, and what he found there was beautiful.

"Honora..." he breathed. A question. A plea.

She rose from her stool and approached the bed slowly. She brought her hand to his face, caressed his skin in gentle circles. "Ash."

How strange. It was all there in her eyes, every emotion he'd thought her incapable of, every ounce of heart and passion that he'd only ever glimpsed in bed. It was as though the window he'd always seen through had suddenly opened, and he realized everything had been there all along.

He pulled her down on top of him, covering her mouth, overwhelmed with the need to capture this moment, to consume her newly seen heat. She responded in kind, pushing her hands beneath his shirt, her fingers igniting his skin.

He had her nightgown off in a moment, and just as quickly his own clothing in a heap on the floor. He pulled her atop him, his hands roving her body, glorying in the silk of her skin. With a sharp movement she brought him inside her and he gasped, grasping her bottom.

It was over quickly, her movements, the tight heat of her easily bringing him to the edge. He cried out, arched against her as she continued to grind against him. When he was spent she stopped, still atop him, still holding him inside her. She sought his hand, and greedily pushed his fingers against her, asking for her own release.

Ash watched her face. How could he have thought her cold? She was all fire and fever, her face aglow with it. Her bare breasts shimmered with it. The skin beneath his touch burned with it.

When she came she called out his name, arched against his fingers and his cock still inside her, setting the room afire.

* * *

They didn't speak of it the next morning. They awoke, dressed and quickly broke their fast as though it were any other morning, as though nothing between them had changed. They didn't need words for such a dramatic shift: what had transpired needed no words. They'd gone to bed last night as their old selves and awoken this morning as their new ones. Any discussion was bound to be awkward and superfluous.

He liked that about her, that she hadn't a need to analyze and dissect. She could simply be, complete in herself and the situation.

In any event, they'd other matters at hand, and racing to intercept Margaret and Wesley took precedence. The anger that had banked last night returned in full force, and Ash needed every ounce of his control to stop his brain from picturing Wesley with his sister.

By God, he had let her down. In a morass of his own supposed misery and the injustice of having to marry, he'd never thought to look past himself and see that his only sister was not well. It wasn't a wrong he could rectify: they might be able to stop Wesley from marrying her, but if he'd compromised her—actually put his filthy hands on her—then Ash didn't know what to do.

Of course, she was already compromised, her reputation besmirched, and if word got out, which it always seemed to do, they'd have a hell of a time getting her through it.

He'd do it, though. Somehow. He had to.

"It won't help," Honora said, breaking the silence they'd been riding in for nearly an hour. "Berating yourself," she answered to his silent question. "We both made mistakes in safeguarding Margaret. I saw that she was struggling. I should have devoted more time to her. I am sorry."

Ash exhaled. "No. No, it was me. I've paid her no attention at all. I should have suspected Wesley."

"How? How could you possibly have suspected that he would do something like this? If anything, I should have suspected. I've never liked the man."

Ash grinned. "Are we arguing about who is to blame?"

Honora cocked her head. "Blaming ourselves instead of each other. How novel."

Ash rested his head against the seat and laughed. "So I was right. We have achieved a breakthrough. After last night...?"

Honora held his gaze.

"Are you blushing? Are those pink cheeks I see on you, my dear?"

She tossed a glove at him. "Never!" She laughed. And then more thoughtfully, "Last night was, it was, well..." she trailed off.

"I felt it, too," he said, hearing the huskiness of his own voice. "Our bodies communicate more readily than our words."

"Perhaps we should leave it at that. Perhaps our words will only cloud matters. I would like to continue as we are."

"As would I." She was right. Discussing this newfound thing between them would only likely lead them away from it. For better or worse, theirs was an uncommon bond.

Ash reached over and grasped her chin, tilting her face closer to his all while holding her gaze. He smiled, and kissed her. With a soft sigh she leaned into him, willing, warm.

And then the carriage jerked to a halt, and the sounds of shouting came from outside.

CHAPTER FIFTEEN

They were fortuitously in time to stop Margaret and Wesley from marrying. Margaret, she later informed them, had quickly begun to experience regret over her impetuous elopement, and had been slowing down Wesley as best she could, knowing that Ash could not be far behind her. Claiming one or two indispositions had been enough to delay them so that Ash and Honora could overtake them at the dismal inn in which they were lodged.

Ash burst in, sending the old wooden door slamming into the wall with a bang. Honora followed closely behind, as the startled looks from the few patrons inside bounced from him to her. Wesley had the misfortune of standing near a window in the taproom, exposed and with nowhere to hide. His face went white at the sight of Ash and he stepped backward, straight into the wall.

"Damn your soul!" Ash grabbed the nearest thing, a shoddy old chair, and hurled it at the other man. Wesley ducked and the chair shattered against the wall behind him.

"Wait!" Honora grabbed Ash's arm, grasping him tight until he looked down at her, and Wesley visibly sagged in relief.

"You can't mean to stop me from thrashing him!" he snarled.

"No!" Honora shook her head. "Only, let the others move out of the way. They've done nothing." The other men seated in the taproom grabbed up their drinks and rushed quickly from their seats to the other side of the room, grateful to be out of the line of fire, but not fearful enough to leave the room and miss the spectacle.

"Are you mad?" Wesley sputtered, his eyes dancing left and right, desperately searching for something to shelter him from the enraged earl.

"Where is my sister?" Ash shouted, throwing a tankard at Wesley. All the while he slowly, steadily approached the cowering man.

"I am here." Her voice came from the stairs, soft, unsteady. She stepped down into the room, unkempt and tired-looking, but not visibly harmed. At least, there were no marks upon her. Honora rushed to Margaret's side for a quick embrace and closer look. Honora met Ash's gaze and nodded, letting him know that there was no immediate threat to her physical well-being.

Ash turned his attention back to Wesley, who'd taken shelter behind a flimsy table. "You greedy, stupid bastard. What the devil were you thinking? Or were you even thinking at all?"

Wesley smirked. "Easy words from the high and mighty Earl of Ashland. You, with your rich wife and title. What do you know of it?"

"You're a fool."

"Spare me!" he spat, the resentment and the scorn he held for Ash very clear. "Why shouldn't I have what you have? She's ruined anyway," he tossed his head at Margaret, who made a keening sound in response and sagged against Honora. "Let us go through with the marriage. It is the best possible outcome."

And then the jackass slid a knife out of his boot, slowly, never breaking eye contact with Ash. He flashed him a grin of victory and stepped toward the stairwell where Honora and Margaret still stood. In a quick movement he reached them.

Ash jerked forward, halted when Wesley raised the knife, its sharp blade gleaming in the shadowy taproom as he twisted it. The onlookers made a shocked sound but hung back. He wasn't pointing the weapon at the women, yet, but he clearly had no reluctance to do so. His eyes never left Ash.

"Enough." Ash tried to keep his voice level and calm, no easy feat with the fury that gripped him. He held up his hands, urging calm, when what he really wanted was to wrap them around Wesley's miserable throat and squeeze until he could squeeze no more.

Honora gripped Margaret's hand, watching Wesley darkly. It was just the way she'd looked at that man Pearson, on that long ago day when he'd questioned her abilities. She may have even directed the look at Ash once or twice.

Ash's heart pounded in his chest. Wesley was undoubtedly stupid enough to harm one of the women in retaliation, or as a means of getting what he wanted. Ash was damned if he'd let him succeed.

Honora moved a step down, putting herself in front of Margaret and directly before Wesley and his waving knife. "No, miss!" One of the spectators cautioned. Ash's heart jumped into his throat. It took everything in him to hold back, but he was afraid that a movement from him would cause Wesley to use the knife.

"How much?" she asked, impassive, dead-calm, watching Wesley with a look of open disgust.

Wesley cocked his head and smiled coldly. "What now?"

"How much money do you want to leave Margaret alone?"

Wesley shook his head. "There isn't any amount you could give me, love. I could take your money once, or I can marry the sister here, take her dowry and as a part of the family, be comfortable for life. No, there's nothing you could give me now." His teeth gleamed white as he grinned, so very pleased with himself.

"So you propose to kidnap Lady Margaret and force her to marry you? How will you stop Ashland?"

"I imagine I'll take you both along, as collateral. If Ash follows, I'll have to test the sharpness of this knife. Perhaps it's a good measure of his affection for you, old girl. That is to say, how genuine can his bond to a grubby *tradeswoman* be? Shall we find out?"

Ash shook with suppressed rage, the urge to violence coursing through him. "There is no way in hell I will let you leave here with either my sister or my wife." He kept his eyes on Wesley's knife, thinking desperately how to get them out of the situation. He needed only to find a way to overpower him, to get Honora and Margaret out of danger and then beat Wesley to a pulp.

"Let me?" Wesley laughed spitefully. "I do not need your permission. For anything, you sanctimonious bastard!"

Without warning there came a sudden explosion of skirts, profanity and screaming. Ash ducked. Wesley went down with a yelp, his knife flying out of his hand and skidding across the floor. Seizing the moment, Ash leapt for the knife and turned to Honora.

"Are you hurt? Are you bleeding?" He ran his hands over her, but could find no signs of a wound.

"I'm fine," she gasped, grasping his hands, clutching them to her chest. "I am unhurt."

"Margaret?" His sister had fled up the stairs, and gingerly made her way down again.

"I am fine." She looked startled and scared, far younger than her nineteen years. Ash reached out and wrapped his arms around her, relief pounding through him.

"What happened?" Ash asked, confounded. Wesley was still prostrate on the floor, curled up and whimpering. The taproom patrons hung back at the edges of the room, wide-eyed.

"I kicked him," Honora declared. "In between the legs."

He looked at Honora, astounded.

"Why, you didn't think Granny would leave me unprepared for an attack? She taught me how to disarm a man when I was twelve." She raised her skirts and extended a foot—a foot clad in the sturdy black boot Ash had charmed from the maid at the ball they'd fled all those weeks ago. "I knew these would prove useful!"

Ash looked down at Wesley, clutching his privates, then at Margaret, pale and shaky, and finally back at Honora. "I'll be damned."

* * *

Ash bought a round for the spectators, who hurried back to their seats to discuss the events they'd witnessed. Taking a still-moaning Wesley by the lapels, he dragged him outside where, with great satisfaction, Ash delivered a bit of his own retribution. "You're a lying dog, Wesley," Ash said into the other man's ear. "I'm sorry I ever called you my friend. If you tell anyone what you've done, or come near my sister or wife, I will flay you alive." He gave him a hard shake, making sure that Wesley felt the warning deep in his aching bones, Ash released him and walked away without a backwards glance.

They departed as quickly as they could. Once in the carriage, and after a lengthy bout of tears, Ash and Honora were able to glean the details of the failed elopement from Margaret.

"The season has been nothing at all like Mother p-promised!" Margaret blew her nose. "It's been perfectly awful. I hadn't made the splash I thought I would. Oh, I know it sounds so silly, but I'd envisioned it being so different. It was like," she looked up, her tear-stained face forlorn, "it was as if I weren't even there. And then Wesley came along, and he was so charming and attentive…"

Ash shifted in his seat, not sure if he wanted to hear what else she had to say.

"He was kind to you," Honora finished, and Margaret started to cry all over again. She and Ash shared a guilty look. His sister had been neglected and ripe for Wesley's manipulations. He pinched the bridge of his nose.

"I am sorry, Margaret, dear." Honora, again. "I guessed you were feeling at odds and I should have made more time for you." She bit her lip and reached over to squeeze Margaret's hand. "You don't have to participate in the Season any longer, if you don't wish to."

"It might not be a choice," Ash said. Margaret looked at him in misery, fat tears trailing down her cheeks. "If word of this debacle has gotten out, you won't be welcome anywhere. I regret being so blunt, but we must face matters as they are."

"Are you certain he won't speak of it?" Honora asked.

"As certain as I can be. I threatened him and he has nothing to gain at this point." Ash did not completely believe this: Wesley had just proven himself to be boundlessly malicious. He might smear Margaret's character simply out of pettiness. Ash had warned him, verbally and physically, but really, there was no telling what the bastard might do.

Margaret appeared uncertain. "You won't f-force me to marry him?"

Ash drew a breath. The idea sickened him, but it might end up being the only way to salvage his sister's reputation. Wesley knew what he was doing.

"No." Honora interjected, her tone brooking no denial. "You will not marry him if you do not wish it, Margaret. You may lose your reputation, but you will not lose our support. You can retire to the country, or go abroad, or do any number of things but I will not let that man take away your choices. There is more to life than the opinion of the *ton*."

Margaret erupted in a fresh bout of tears, although these were ones of relief. She sagged against Honora, who patted her and made soothing sounds. And Ash... An emotion built inside Ash's chest that he didn't know what to do with, so he stared at the window and said nothing.

They rested at the same inn they'd stopped at on the way, acquiring a small room for Margaret and a slightly larger chamber for themselves. After dinner, they all retired immediately, exhausted by the events of the past few days and wondering what awaited them in London.

Ash and Honora were quiet as they prepared for bed.

After stripping to his drawers, he sat on the bed. Ash cleared his throat. "I want to thank you."

Honora sat on a small stool, brushing her hair. "Whatever for?"

"For going after Margaret as you did. For caring for her."

She stopped brushing, turning to stare at her lap with her face closed up. He thought she might be overcome with emotion, but when she finally looked up at him, he could see she was incensed.

"Of course I would go after her! Did you think I wouldn't?"

Ash didn't know what to say, startled by her fierce reaction.

She tossed the brush onto the table with a clatter. "Will you ever consider me a part of this family?"

"You are," he replied tentatively. "Of course you are."

"No," she shook her head. "I am not. Not with James, not with your mother. You thank me for going after Margaret—would I do any less for a sister of my own blood?"

Ash chose his words carefully. "I did not mean what I said. About James. About you, and being family. I only wanted to prove that I could handle that situation without advice or guidance. I wanted to show that I was capable. I was wrong to say what I said."

Honora actually looked fairly astounded, her mouth even gaped the tiniest bit. Just enough so that he could glimpse the edge of her tongue, a sight that did delightful things to his cock. He shifted on the bed, lest she notice any inopportune movement beneath his drawers.

"I suppose I was a bit overbearing in my reaction to those events." She said it as if it physically pained her, pronouncing each word slowly and painfully, and Ash had to laugh. He rubbed a hand over his face, his tired eyes, his raspy beard. It had been an exhausting day. At any point the tension could have worked against them, perhaps even carried them irreparably away from one another. The fact that it hadn't nearly made him giddy.

"You are so eminently capable, Honora. There seems to be nothing you can't manage and it does make me wonder where that leaves me? What use do you have for me?"

She stared at him, puzzled.

"James is my brother. I'm sure you could have had the boy's undying loyalty and the entire situation resolved within half an hour, but I knew I was capable of handling this one matter."

Honora spoke slowly. "Were you proving it to me, or to yourself?"

The question gave him pause. "Both, I think. I think I needed to show myself, as much as you."

Faint sounds came from downstairs, patrons enjoying themselves. The room was cozy, small and warm with a cheery fire. The bed linens were soft and clean. They'd drawn the curtains over the window, shutting out the black, chill night.

"You know," Ash said, "I can't think of anywhere I'd rather be at this moment."

Honora stilled, tipped her head and regarded him. He leaned back against the stacked pillows, crossing his arms behind his head.

"I've come to enjoy your presence, wife." He spoke the words lightly, belying the weight they carried.

"A shocking turn of events!" she mocked, not without amusement.

"Well. It is, when you consider the inauspicious beginnings of our union. We could have easily grown to despise one another. Instead, we…"

Honora waited, brows raised, silently challenging him to finish his thought. But he didn't know how to finish it. What were they, exactly? Not like anyone of his acquaintance. The married couples he knew mostly tolerated one another, and only barely. He and Honora had developed something that was like a friendship with lust. Was that what a successful marriage was? "We have formed a rather unique bond." She grimaced, letting him know how unsatisfactory she found his response.

"That we have." She glanced down, hiding her eyes. "Though we cannot articulate why or how. We seem to communicate best physically."

Well, now he was definitely growing hard and he didn't bother to hide it. She lifted her gaze and swept it over him, quickly, and then turned to the fire. "Come now," he said, the blaze moving into his chest, his throat, his heart. "Don't be a coward and look away."

She flung her gaze back to him, taking the challenge as he knew she would. Her cheeks were pink, her eyes shone. He could see each breath she took in the rise and fall of her chest.

"Take off your nightgown."

A heavy breath escaped her, a sound of surprise and desire. She watched him for a moment and then stood, while her hands slowly moved to the row of buttons below her neck. She undid each one with infinite care, never breaking his gaze. Ash was awash in lust, it coursed through every inch of him, lit a fire down his spine and outward. Hell, even his toes tingled.

"Do you know," he rasped, "I watched you once, in the bath. I spied upon you from a crack in my door." He moved his hand downward, into the waistband of his drawers and grasped himself. "I watched your maid help you disrobe, saw you unwrapped like the most erotic gift I'd ever seen. You rubbed your breasts. And then you bent over and I saw what a truly spectacular backside you had." He moved his hand, up and down, pushing himself into a frenzy. The memory of that moment. The sight of her now.

Honora licked her lips, a slow, purposeful gesture that fully conveyed her arousal. She finished with the damned buttons and pushed off the nightgown. The white linen cascaded over her luminescent skin, leaving her naked, backlit by the fire. She cupped her breasts and caressed the sharp, pink points.

"Is that what you did, when you watched me? Did you touch yourself?"

"I did," he breathed.

"Take off your drawers," she commanded. "I want to see."

He almost spilled then and there. Drawing on every reserve of control, he did as she asked, pushing his undergarment down off his hips. "I await your command."

"Keep going." She continued to rub her nipples, circling them with her thumbs.

Ash followed her direction, grasping himself firmly and moving quickly, with intent. She groaned and bit her lip. The tension spooled within Ash. "I can't… I won't last long…"

She moved onto the bed and kneeled beside him. Without a sound she bent over him and took him in her mouth. Ash arched against the heat of her, against the unexpectedness of it, against her mouth on him for the first time.

"Oh, God. Oh, God." He clasped her head, moved against her.

She reached beneath him and cupped him and it was over; he exploded. His vision went dark, the breath left his body. He arched as he came, as everything inside him folded over into the pleasure of his release. He probably screamed her name.

When it was over, he could barely speak. She cuddled against him, bringing the counterpane over them. She rested her head on his chest, her hand against her heart. She bent her leg over his, and moved against him once. "Don't worry. We have all night." And then he was asleep.

* * *

He woke some time later and made it up to her, bringing her to pleasure with a relentless focus that had her begging for mercy, taking her with his mouth before spreading her wide open and having her completely. It was Honora's turn for speechlessness and she collapsed against him, gladly enclosed by his limbs, his warmth beneath her cheek, his skin flush against hers.

He rose at some point for a drink of water. She peeked at him, his perfect form, and not for the first time was glad he was so active. He crawled back into bed, handing her the glass so that she, too, could drink. "I can't risk you swooning on me," he teased.

She nestled back into him and they continued to talk. Honora told him about Pearson and the disloyalty of men who'd known her for years, about missing the investor's meeting she'd worked so hard to arrange. He made a low sound, like a tiny growl, as she told him, angered on her behalf.

She was finally able to ask him more about the trip with James. He updated her, telling her the boy had remained recalcitrant while his mother had been beside herself.

"She'd no idea he had left school and come to confront me, as you guessed. I think she was fairly mortified at his behavior. But," he laughed, "you can be assured that he lost that resentful smirk in his mother's presence. I would have cuffed him, myself, but she was torn between tears and affection. I do hope our children end up with more sense."

A feeling akin to stepping into a hot bath overtook Honora. A pleasure-born blush suffused her entire body, singeing her skin and the place in her chest that held her heart, and for a second she could not breathe, so deep was her delight. It was not simply his mention of children, but the offhand, matter-of-fact nature of his comment, conjuring up images of daughters and sons with his looks and her brains. Fortunately, Ash went on with his story, not expecting a response, for Honora was momentarily too addled to speak.

"She made him apologize to me, and said he'd be writing a letter to you, Mother and Margaret for his bad manners and temerity. She... she seems to be raising them well."

Honora reached for his hand, loosely lacing his fingers with hers. She knew it wasn't an easy admission.

"I told him, James, that is," Ash continued. "During our ride, I told him that I could understand his anger, and that I hoped he realized one day that it was our father he was angry with, and not me. Not really."

"He must know that," Honora said. "In some way."

"Perhaps. Although he might never acknowledge it."

They were quiet for a while, lost in their thoughts, enjoying their closeness. After a while, Ash spoke, almost as an afterthought.

"I think we should have them at Ashland. After the repairs."

Honora lifted her head, amazed. "But your Mother—"

"My mother won't have to be there, if she is offended. But I think we must maintain the connection. They are family, after all. I won't ignore them. And the children...well, they are children, and if we can help them, then we must."

"I think that is a wonderful idea." She lowered her head and pressed a light kiss to his chest, pleased with his gesture.

She drifted against him, a light and soft sleep of lingering pleasure. After some time, a thought woke her and she found her voice enough to whisper against the even rise and fall of his chest. "I know what this is, Ash. Between us."

He made a small questioning sound, his hand tracing idly over her back.

"This is love!"

And she closed her eyes, smiling at his sharp inhalation of shock.

EPILOGUE

"**A**shland! Ashland! Do watch where you are going!"

It was too late. The boys, certainly possessed of some sixth sense regarding foodstuffs, had not only noticed the confectioner's shop but had already made their way inside. Honora could see little Henry's face pressing up against the glass display case, devouring the cakes with his eyes, while his elder brother Samuel hopped on one foot beside him in an agony of anticipation.

Ash looked her way and shrugged, and with a grin followed the boys inside.

Honora sighed. Her hope to present clean, well-mannered children to her mother-in-law vanished. Mother Ashland would take one look at her untidy grandsons, whom the confectioner was already plying with assorted sticky and messy items, and give Honora that familiar gaze of disappointment tinged with disbelief.

Honora laughed. "It's not as if I was going to please her, is it Thomas?" she asked the baby in her arms, giving him a little jiggle. "Mama will never please Grandmother, no matter how long she's been away in America." She kissed the baby's face and he squealed in delight, making Honora laugh again.

After several years away from society, Margaret had eventually married an American who fell head over heels in love with her and in his typical, blithe American way, hadn't the slightest concern for social scandals. He'd taken Margaret to live in New York, and Mother Ashland had mercifully taken to dividing her time between England and the United States.

Now, after nearly six months away, the dowager, accompanied by Margaret and her husband, had just returned to England, and Ash and Honora had decided to enjoy the fair day and walk with the boys to pay them their welcome visit. Honora should have anticipated chocolates along the way, thinking, not for the first time, that her children should be dressed exclusively in shades of black to disguise their inevitable grubbiness.

In a few weeks they would decamp to the country. For the first time, they would all be under the roof of Ashland Park together. The *intact* roof, Honora liked to point out. Ash and Honora and their boys, Margaret and her brood, and Mother Ashland would all be in residence at the freshly restored and fully functioning ancestral seat. It was nothing short of a miracle, Honora often thought, that the place hadn't at any point actually fallen about their ears. Well, most of it, she amended; the old east wing *had* actually fallen down about their ears.

But Ashland had taken that project in hand, had devoted himself over the past years to the manor's restoration, and had succeeded admirably. He'd shown skill with the old place, taking particular pride in the installation of a modern bathing chamber between their bedrooms. It was his favorite room of the house. It was, he liked to remind her, where this baby in her arms had come into being.

He'd fulfilled a promise, too, and had his brothers to visit at Ashland Park. There were initially a lot of terse silences and frowns, but eventually Ash had come to a sort of understanding with James and Jonathan, and they had achieved a civil relationship.

Ashland and the boys exited the confectioner's shop, loaded down with treats. Young Henry had jam smeared across his mouth and Samuel had chocolate in his hair. She wasn't sure how they dirtied themselves so quickly, or so thoroughly. Really, it was an art form. Even Ash has powdered sugar on his chin.

He was watching her as she glanced up, all of her exasperation vanishing at the look in his eye. A small smile tugged at the corner of his mouth and like that, heat pooled in Honora's center and her breath came fast and she wished they were alone. Just like that. Three babies and five years of marriage had done nothing to quell her desire. His smile grew, became a knowing smirk and Honora blushed—actually blushed. It was still like that.

The noisy crowd around them faded away.

He stepped over to her, the boys in tow, and took Thomas from her arms, watching her all the while, his features familiar but no less intoxicating—even more fascinating, because now they were beloved. The quirk of his lip, his blue green gaze, his open and easy manner—all of it cherished familiarity. Honora sighed and leaned in, unable to resist pressing a kiss to his cheek over baby Thomas's head.

She recognized the small sound he made, knew it for the reciprocated wealth of love and desire, and smiled, full of contentment, and joy.

He raised his hand to caress her cheek, looking down at her with tenderness.

"Wife," he said, and Honora smiled, and answered as she always did.

"Yes, my love."

THE END

ACKNOWLEDGEMENTS

Writing a book is hard. I couldn't have done it without the constant encouragement of my beta reader, co-author and real-life super friend, Elizabeth Kingston. Laura Kinsale is an incredibly kind and generous person whose influence is invaluable. Janice for reading my stuff, even though she doesn't read romance. Monica for such enthusiastic support. And the Dining Club, may she soon ride again.

And my family, my heart.

THANK YOU

Thank you for reading. Please consider leaving an honest review of this book at a site such as Amazon or Goodreads. Reviews are very helpful to independent authors such as myself, and very much appreciated.

ALSO BY SUSANNA MALCOLM

BESOTTED WITH THE VISCOUNT

THE MISADVENTURES OF A TITIAN-HAIRED GODDESS & AN OUTRAGEOUS HELLION, an affectionate parody of historical romance, co-authored with Elizabeth Kingston.

ABOUT THE AUTHOR

Susanna Malcolm has been reading romance since she was far too young to be doing so. She lives near Chicago with her family and no pets, although there are rabbits in the yard.

Visit her at:
www.SusannaMalcolm.com
Twitter: @SusannaMalcolm
Facebook.com/SusannaMalcolmAuthor
Instagram:
www.instagram.com/susannamalcolm/

Sign up for my (infrequent & brief yet delightful) newsletter on my website!

Made in the USA
Columbia, SC
23 August 2021

44163380R00176